What He Wants

Baxter Boys, Volume 1

Jessie Gussman

Published by Jessie Gussman, 2018.

This is a work of fiction. Similarities to real people, places, or events are entirely coincidental.

WHAT HE WANTS

First edition. December 27, 2018.

Copyright © 2018 Jessie Gussman.

Written by Jessie Gussman.

In February of 2013 I sat on our couch and slapped my laptop shut, muttering in frustration, "Anyone could write a better book than that."

My husband paused as he walked through the room, on his way to check our maple sap that was boiling just outside in the chill of early evening. "Then do it," he said.

Ha.

It is possible that if I had not met my husband I might have still written a book. But not this book.

It is with a humble heart, full of gratitude, that I dedicate Torque's story to my husband and best friend.

No greater love hath any man than this, that a man lay down his life for his friends.

Chapter 1

Cassidy Kimball stood on the cement sidewalk and faced the red brick Pennsylvania state penitentiary building. Hot July sunlight glinted off the razor wire that looped in circles at the top and beside the chain-link fence. Off to the right, the circular guard house, with its tinted windows, glared down at the parched brown and empty exercise yard.

Her stomach twisted like mangled metal in a car accident.

It could have been her on the inside. Not here, of course. But somewhere.

She glanced at her watch before dragging her clammy hands down her skirt. *Please, God, don't let my makeup melt before he walks out.* A simple request; she shouldn't care what her makeup looked like, although right now, it felt like much-needed armor. Plus, she'd learned the hard way to be thankful for little things.

And big things. Like not serving the ten-year prison sentence for vehicular homicide that should have been hers after she T-boned a car with Torque Baxter's pickup when she was nineteen. Nope, she didn't serve it. Because Torque was serving, had served, it for her.

Hot and turbulent doubt swirled in her stomach. Would he see what she had become and think his sacrifice had been worth it?

Part of her wanted to announce her sacrifices to him, to tell him of her charity work and the people she helped. That he had played the gallant knight in shining armor to her Cowardly Lion, but that it had not been in vain. Part of her wanted him to see it for himself. All of her craved his approval. Or maybe just his forgiveness.

Swallowing the nerves that clenched her throat, Cassidy twisted the delicate linked gold of her wristwatch. Any minute now. Would she still recognize him? Of course, she would. The question was, would he recognize all that she had done as a tiny down payment on the huge debt she owed him?

She reached the same conclusion she had every day for the last ten years. There was nothing she could do to pay back her monstrous obligation. There was no way to atone for the cowardice that she had shown. How could she have been so yellow?

When he'd seen the passengers in the other car, when he'd known what the consequences were going to be, he'd never wavered. His brown eyes had been steady and level as he said, "Get out of here and don't look back. You don't know anything about this." She hadn't understood at first what he was going to do. Still shaken from the accident, she'd not really been thinking straight. But she hadn't needed her brain to be fully functioning to know that she was in deep trouble. She'd already been fighting the urge to run. His command had prompted her to do what she subconsciously wanted to. "Hurry, before anyone comes."

Then, he hadn't accepted her calls, hadn't graced her visits with his presence, hadn't used the money she deposited in his account. Her letters returned unopened, and her emails disappeared into the prison of cyberspace. She didn't know, couldn't know, what he thought or felt.

She assumed he hated her.

A bead of sweat trickled down her temple. Her watch chain snapped under her shaking fingers. She shoved the broken links into her clutch.

Her hands stilled as the prison door opened. The jaws of a monster spitting out its prey. Prey she had fed it.

A man, tall and straight, strode out into the sunlight. Her eyes devoured him. Same casual arrogance dressed in jeans and a t-shirt. Same confident walk, with only a slight limp. The limp was her fault, too. With his slim build, Torque would never be bulky, but she could see the t-shirt that probably fit him when he first walked into this building as an almost-eighteen-year-old now stretched tight over shoulders that had widened and filled out.

Cassidy bit her lip and lifted her chin, taking a deep breath to calm the cramping of her stomach and disguise the curl of heat that came to life in her chest. Torque had always had that effect on her. She pushed the feeling aside and channeled her inner upper-crust snob—the only defense that had ever come close to working against the elemental pull that Torque exerted on her.

The last words that man had said to her were, "Shut up, Cassidy." Now, she intended to get one question answered. Then she had to figure out how to pay him back. What did ten years of a man's life cost?

TORQUE FLOATED ABOVE the sidewalk, taking in big lungfuls of the sweetest smelling air in the country. Same air that he'd been breathing for the last decade, but it smelled different on this side of the fence. Felt different, too. He wanted to lie belly-down and kiss the ground. He resisted the urge.

Instead he exalted in the unchaining of his spirit, in the freedom and openness that surrounded him, in the beautiful blue sky, in the purple mountains of his home state unobscured by fences or bars.

His stomach rumbled.

A small talon of anxiety poked his rib. He'd have to find his own meal tonight. After years of his basic needs being met on a schedule with no thought of his own being necessary... He pushed the thought away. He'd taken care of himself for years before he went up. It was a privilege to do so again. He couldn't think of it any other way. He certainly was not going to worry about it. There were things that, to him, were more important than eating, anyway.

Before he'd been locked up, he'd been well on his way to his goal of owning his own diesel garage. But technology had moved on without him. A few outdated Popular Mechanics weren't enough to update his knowledge of emissions standards and computerized motors. Still, surely there was some diesel garage that would hire a hard worker and a quick learner. With a rap sheet.

First things first. He scanned the sidewalk for his brother Turbo or at least a monster pickup that would be Turbo's latest project. All he saw was a slender woman in a slim skirt with miles of legs reaching down to impossibly high heels. She stood at the T in the sidewalk. Long brown hair streaked with blond. Big shades. Not Turbo.

He didn't allow his eyes to linger. Beautiful women had been few and far between in the lockup. But he wasn't going there, although his eyes were drawn to this one like air to the intake valve. He had a life to put back together first.

She stood with one hip jutted out. A hand with shiny red nails rested on it. Her whole bearing screamed money and class.

Most definitely not for him.

He altered his direction, aiming to give her a good ten-foot birth on the right without being obvious about avoiding her. His infatuation with one such girl was how he had landed in the pen to begin with.

Infatuation.

No. Chivalry.

Whatever. It would have driven him to step between her and a bullet. That would have been a heck of a lot faster than what he actually did, which was put himself in her place, and *she had allowed it*. He'd told her to. He'd volunteered to do it. He'd kept his word and protected her through it all. That was great. But his sacrificing days were done. Not going down that road again.

The woman casually removed her shades.

Torque's heart rammed to a stop the way a rod shot through the side of a block kills an engine.

Cassidy.

What was she doing here? All his body systems slammed into overdrive.

He clenched his jaw and kept walking. He'd be ready to face her when he had put his life back together. When he could meet her on equal footing, and she no longer looked down her cute, rich-girl's nose at him.

Who was he kidding? Like he'd ever be good enough.

Turbo had to be around here somewhere. *Please, God*. Another sweep of the visitors' parking lot revealed only a low-slung, red sports car.

Mere feet from Cassidy, he surrendered to the inevitable and stopped. Her scent overwhelmed him. Exotic fruit. The memory of a hot summer night slammed into him. Radio on. Cruising. Country air blowing into his truck and tangling with the incense of the girl next to him. Suddenly the urge to turn and run surged through him. Back into the prison, back where the smell of perfume and the twitch of a lip didn't turn his brain to mush and make him do the stupidest thing a man had ever done for a woman, back to where his brain and heart weren't engaged in all-out warfare and where it would be easy to remember the only smart choice he needed to make: stay away from Cassidy.

Those soft red lips, the ones he'd dreamed about for years, the ones he'd heard later that same night scream in terror, opened. "Why'd you take my place, Torque?"

Torque schooled his features, refusing to allow the longing her voice elicited to show on his face. Rich, yet friendly, living in her mansion on the hill, Cassidy had infatuated him since this poor, trailer-park trash saw her in the kindergarten lunch line. He had plenty of experience in shoving that magnetic attraction aside and pretending indifference.

He didn't have to fake the bitterness.

"Didn't hear you on the witness stand contradicting my story."

"You told me to shut up."

"Has to be the first time in your life you listened to anyone." Was that hurt that flickered across her features? Couldn't be. Not Cassidy. Tough as tempered steel. "You've got a mouth, and I've never seen you afraid to use it."

"My dad wouldn't let me."

Torque snorted. What a line of crap. "Your dad wouldn't let you ride with me either. But that didn't stop you." Heat spread up his side as he remembered how she felt snuggled up against him on the bench seat, her hair whipping in the wind, her laughing eyes and flashing teeth grinning up at him. Her hand clenching his leg. For that one short ride, he'd forgotten that she was rich and he poor and that their futures, headed in completely opposite directions, would never merge into one.

But where he'd been since then wasn't so easily wiped away, and he allowed his heart to harden. She was tempered steel. He was titanium. She would break first. This time.

"After the accident, it was different. He wouldn't let me out of his sight until you..." Her voice trailed off, and she looked away.

"Until I was locked up?" he asked with a sardonic lift to his brow. He wanted to close the step between them and take her in his arms. Not that she needed it or wanted it. It was simply the effect she always had on him, like there was a vulnerability to her that no one but him could see, and it brought out every protective instinct in his body. He hated himself for it. He hated her even more.

"Yeah," she whispered. A breeze lifted her hair, showcasing the elegant curve of her neck. She turned her head, and he looked away.

"Plus, you had given the police a lie. I wasn't going to contradict that without talking to you." Her chin tilted. "You wouldn't talk to me."

She visited the jail once, where he was being held, unable to make bail. Strutting down the corridor in her designer clothes amid catcalls and whistles from the other inmates, looking like she belonged on a Paris runway rather than visiting a good-for-nothing like him, surrounded by all the other lawbreakers and criminals locked up in that dump. He'd taken one look at her and turned away, refusing to speak to her. But it was then that he solidified the impulsive decision he made the night of the accident. She didn't belong in there. And as much as he couldn't decide whether he loved her or hated her, he could at least protect her from that.

His dad might have been a lousy parent with even worse child-naming skills, who eventually ran off, but his mother and grandmother had instilled a rock-solid code of ethics in his brain. Women deserve protection. They might not want it. They might not need it. Still. A woman nurtures, a man protects. And with Cassidy, and the hold she had on his over-hormoned teenaged brain...heck, he hadn't used his brain at all to make that decision.

But with that choice—the choice to become a convicted criminal—went the last hope he harbored that he might eventually be able to knock on the door of her mansion and speak to her father as an equal, seeking and receiving permission to date his daughter.

He couldn't let her see his weakness. He couldn't articulate his reasons then, and he wasn't sure he wanted to now. He changed the subject instead. "Well, it's been fun, getting reacquainted and all, but Turbo's gonna be here any minute." Torque stepped toward the parking lot.

"He's not coming."

Torque stopped midstride. His stomach sank like water in oil, a slow, graceful, unstoppable dive to his feet.

"I told him I'd bring you home." She spoke to his back.

Turbo owned his own truck and was busy, of course, but Torque hadn't thought that would abandon him to Cassidy. Of course, Turbo didn't know how twisted his feelings for her were, either.

Steeling himself against the idea of spending the next three hours cooped up in a car with Cassidy, he turned back. "The last time I rode with you isn't in my top ten best memories."

Did she flinch? Had to be his imagination.

He wasn't angry at her. Not really. And he didn't hate her. But he still wanted to insist that he drive, wanted to dominate her because of the inferiority complex she always brought out in him, but his license was long expired. Just one thing on a long list of things for him to take care of.

Cassidy stepped closer and put one shiny red fingernail on his chest where it scalded like acid through his t-shirt. He couldn't have moved or looked away from her blue-black gaze even if his shirt had incinerated from his body.

"I asked you why you lied. Why you took my place. Why you served the time that should have been mine."

He stared over her shoulder. There was no way he was going there.

Her minty breath flowed over his face. "Torque, I owe you. I don't know what ten years are worth, I'm not sure you can put a price tag on them, but I have to do something to pay you."

This obligation that she felt didn't sit right. The feelings that he wanted from her were much deeper and more intimate.

He didn't want her to owe him, *he wanted her to love him.*

Stepping away from her dagger of a finger, he started walking again. "I don't want anything from you."

"Torque..." Her heels clicked on the pavement as she hurried after him. The red sports car was hers. Had to be.

The "Bus Stop" sign caught his eye. He fingered the small amount of money in his pocket. A small sliver of anxiety slipped through him. It had been so long since he'd done anything for himself. Getting on a bus, paying the fare... Another burst of anxiety, thicker and heavier, tore through his chest.

Suddenly the fresh air, the wide-open space, the looming mountains in the distance, all seemed too big, too much, too threatening.

He set his jaw, refusing to give in to the sudden insecurity. He wouldn't ride with Cassidy. He'd take the bus, prove that he could do it.

"Torque!"

He swung around, realizing that Cassidy had said his name several times, and he'd been so caught up in the grip of anxiety and borderline panic, he'd not even heard her. He hadn't expected to have that kind of trouble adjusting to life on the outside.

Setting his feet, he crossed his arms over his chest. "Yeah?" he asked, grateful his voice didn't crack and hoping his face didn't show the anxiety that still curled in his chest.

"This is my car." She indicated the beat-up dark blue clunker beside him.

Surprise shot through him. He tried to cover it, but his eyes ripped back to her, the skyscraper heels, the fancy blouse and classic skirt. The perfect hair and makeup. It all screamed money and class. But the car?

"I'm taking the bus." He turned. Whatever her deal, he really didn't want any part of it. If he kept telling himself that, he might start to believe it.

"Torque, wait."

He stopped but didn't turn.

"Listen, I know you're angry for what happened..."

"Not at what happened. And I'm not angry," he said through clenched teeth.

"Great imitation," she said, half under her breath.

He spun. Couldn't stop himself from taking a step toward her, reaching out, and grabbing her forearm. "I had enough time in the last ten years to figure out I was just a toy for you. Something you played with when you were bored with your high-society life. I get it." He dropped her arm like it had erupted in hot grease. Her skin felt soft and warm and alive under his fingers. Fingers that hadn't seen much human contact and definitely not the softness of a woman in the last ten years. He shut his mouth, clenched his fist, and stomped off.

"I'm your sponsor."

He skidded to a stop. Turned slowly. "No," he said drawing the word out even as he racked his brain for where he might be wrong. "I served my whole sentence. Every day of it. I'm out, free and clean. No parole. No stipulations."

"It's a new program. Officially called the Reintegration into Society Sponsorship Program, it's designed to help people who have been in prison for a while readjust to society, find or keep a job, update on the latest technology, brush up their skill sets, that type of thing. It pairs a professional with a former, uh, inmate."

He smirked as she stumbled over the word. Like she didn't know what to call him. "Ex-con. Pairs a 'professional,'" he said it in a jeering tone, "with an ex-con." Then he snorted at the irony. "Do they know they paired this ex-con with the 'professional' who should have been in prison in the first place?"

"No." Her tone was small, and he felt instant guilt. It had always been his intention to protect her, not hurt her.

He sighed. "I supposed that's what the meeting they told me I had to attend tomorrow is about?"

"Yes. It's a small program, just starting. There are eight pairs, including us."

"So, let me get this straight. You've kept up with diesel mechanics over the last ten years, and you're going to help me catch up and land a job?"

The last time, her tone had been affected, but now, for the first time, her confident carriage seemed to wilt. "It wasn't very fair of me to ask to be paired with you, was it?"

She had asked to be paired with him. To torture him? To rub in his face that he was an ex-con and she wasn't? Or, worse, out of pity?

"This isn't mandatory for me."

"No. Not for you, since you're not out on parole. But," she tilted her proud head, and her eyes almost seemed to plead. "if you were to ever get in any kind of trouble again, this would look good when you came up before the judge."

"Lady, maybe you haven't figured this out, but when that judge looks at me, all he sees is street trash that's better off out of society and behind bars."

"He's wrong."

He wasn't going to fall for her lies. Not a second time. Once, he'd believed she'd seen more in him than anyone else, that he could be successful and climb out of the gutter he'd been born into, where no one expected him to do more than get an entry-level position in some kind of manual labor job and keep it until he retired. Nothing wrong with that, but Cassidy had made him think he could be more.

He could be. He knew it. And he didn't need her to help.

"I'm not planning on getting into trouble again."

"You didn't plan this, either."

He shrugged. She was right about that.

"Listen. I might be able to help, but I need you to do this program."

"Help?" he said derisively. "Like you helped me ten years ago?"

"You told me to leave. If you had given any indication that you wanted anything from me, I would have done everything I could to do what you wanted."

"Big words. Actions don't back 'em up."

"You wouldn't talk to me, wouldn't accept my mail..."

He held a hand up. "Enough."

"You keep acting like this was my fault."

"It was."

Her lips pursed together, and she looked away. He should have felt satisfaction, but he only felt the nagging sense of guilt. Guilt for hurting her. Never mind the last ten years. Guess his heart had missed that part. It had always been on her side.

"You're the one who stole my truck," he said roughly.

"It was hardly stealing."

True. He would have given her his truck to go along with his heart, of course. The problem was he should have taught her how to drive it.

He fingered the money in his pocket. It was all he had in the world. But he wasn't getting in a car with Cassidy. He could work. He could fight. And he'd never quit. But she was his weakness. Always had been. If he were going to get out of the hole he was in now, he needed to keep his distance. She could derail his good intentions with one small touch of her hand.

Once more, he turned to go.

"I'll give you a ride."

"The bus is safer." It was a slam, and she flinched, which did not make him feel better.

She lifted her head, like she was ready to take it on the other cheek. "But you'll come to the meeting tomorrow?"

He stopped but didn't turn around. The rumbling of a motor sounded in the distance. His ride was about to arrive. "I'll think about it." He shouldn't go. Should protect himself with everything he had, but chances were he hadn't learned a thing in the pen, and he'd be there, just because he'd see Cassidy, and he'd never been able to resist that.

Chapter 2

The bus bumped down the highway, swaying as the airbags gave with the pressure of the pothole s in the road. Torque would never have guessed that a bus from Philly to Altoona, PA, would be so crowded.

They hit an exceptionally large hole on the turnpike, and his shoulder brushed the old lady beside him. She'd shrunk up against the window when he'd sat down, but he sat with his boots planted, his hands in his lap in plain sight, and didn't move. That seemed to settle her down after an hour or so.

He stared over her head, out the window at fields of corn and beans, planted in rows as straight as a good man's life. Fields the same now as they were when he'd gone up—a lot younger and a heck of a lot more innocent, despite his rugged upbringing. Part of him resented the time that he'd missed and the innocence that he'd lost. Part of him still wondered if he did the right thing, although he never doubted that he'd do it all over again the same way. His life would never be a straight row, even if what he'd done still felt like the best thing to him. He'd volunteered to take Cassidy's penalty. There was nothing immoral about that; the price had been paid.

The elderly bus driver continued to race along at what felt like a reckless pace to Torque, but it'd been a while since he'd gone any faster than running speed. The Jersey barriers lining the edge of the road flew by at an alarming rate. Torque didn't mind their proximity, though. It was the wide-open spaces that kickstarted the prison-release anxiety.

A bang exploded through the bus, followed by a long, drawn-out hiss. Torque jumped along with everyone else, his heart jumping and his palms in an instant sweat. Someone screamed. Then silence. The bus swayed and dipped as the driver jerked the wheel to the right, pulling off along the narrow shoulder, squeezing up along the cement barriers.

Torque wiped his hands on his jeans. Most likely, an airbag had blown out. Not the kind that everyone else would be familiar with, but the kind that had replaced springs as suspension on all commercial vehicles—trucks and busses. Indeed, as they pulled to a stop, the back of the bus leaned a little toward the passenger side.

The white-haired driver already held his cell phone to his ear. The hissing continued, even after the driver shut the motor off.

A tractor trailer roared by, inches from the window.

"Okay, everyone," the driver announced in a raspy voice. "We have a repairman on his way. Please stay seated as there is no safe place to disembark."

"How soon?" someone shouted from the back.

"Two hours," the driver answered wearily.

Murmurs and complaints followed his announcement.

The driver snapped his seatbelt off. Probably to go put the orange triangles out. Torque debated with himself. Did he really want to draw that kind of attention, by standing up and volunteering to head out? Everyone knew he'd been picked up at the prison, since it had been the last stop.

He hated the insecurity that plagued him since his release two hours ago. Like he wasn't as good as everyone else. Even though he hadn't even done the crime for which he'd served the time. Prison did a good job at beating a man down. Cassidy's mentor program might actually be a good idea.

Without allowing himself another thought, he stood. The bus driver met his eyes in the rearview mirror. He kept his hands in sight—a habit he'd picked up in prison—and started slowly down the aisle.

The driver's brows puckered, and his mouth opened, like he was going to tell Torque to sit back down. Just a few feet from the driver,

Torque spoke, projecting his voice to be heard. "I'll set the triangles up, and I can take a look at it if you want."

"I've got people coming. The police will be here soon, too."

"I'm guessing it's a blown airbag. If you've got a pair of vice grips somewhere on this thing, I can pinch the airline off, so we can at least get down to the nearest exit and park in a safe spot. Maybe somewhere where everyone can get out and stretch their legs?" Torque stopped by the front seat, trying not to crowd the driver. He held his hands up like it didn't matter to him if the driver took him up on it or not.

"What's vice grips gonna do?" the driver asked slowly.

"If it's a blown airbag, the grips won't fix it, but I can pinch the airline off to stop the leak which will give you brakes to make it to the next exit. Wouldn't want to run a hundred miles on it, but won't hurt anything to go a short distance." Torque put a hand on the pole. "Unless you've got eggs in the luggage compartment? Then we'd better stay put." He meant it as a joke. With the airbag out, the suspension would be compromised, and they'd feel every bump.

The driver's lips curved up. "No eggs."

Torque allowed his mouth to curve up, too. It had been a while since he'd shared a little clean humor with another human. It made the ten years he'd spent locked up seem to vanish on one hand, and on the other, he felt like an eighteen-year-old in a twenty-eight-year-old body.

He wasn't a kid anymore. But he'd missed all those experiences from his twenties that should have helped him ease into his thirties. Now, he felt like he was eighteen going on eighty.

He held his hand out to the driver. "Torque Baxter."

The driver looked at it a minute. Torque almost let his hand drop before the old guy placed his gnarled fingers in his. "Bill Anders." He jerked his head. "What'd they lock you up for?"

"Vehicular manslaughter." He didn't bother with the protestations of innocence. He'd pled guilty. The time was served. Every minute of it.

The old man pushed his glasses up on his nose. Another line of tractor trailers whooshed by. His teeth rattled in his mouth. Finally, he wiped a hand down his pants and sighed. "If you can get us off this road, that'll be great." He nodded at a black box beside the shifter. "There's a couple of tools in that box right there."

Torque didn't wait for a second round of permission. He didn't want to get released from prison, only to be killed along the turnpike on the way home, and the way this bus was sitting, so close to the Jersey barriers with no room to move over more, it was about as dangerous as declining a request from the Aryan Brotherhood. Put in that perspective, Torque figured he'd take the bus.

There were no vice grips in the box.

He looked up to see the driver watching him intently. Probably to make sure he didn't steal anything. Irritation rippled around his neck. He closed the box and lifted his hands again, just enough for the driver to see they were empty.

"No grips. Where's the orange triangles?" Every Class A vehicle was required by law to have the triangles and use them in case of a breakdown.

Bill dug them out from behind the seat and handed them to Torque.

"Thanks," Bill said. His face still held a hint of suspicion.

"When the trooper shows up, I'll see if they have the grips. Otherwise, they'd better shut that lane down which'll screw traffic up from here back to Philly."

The driver nodded out the window to the big exit sign one hundred yards down the highway. "It's only two miles to the next exit."

"I'll see what I can do." He stepped out of the bus into the bright fall sunlight. He took a second to lift his face to the sun, closing his eyes, and relish the feel of the heat and breeze. Taking a deep breath, he savored the fall scent mixed with diesel exhaust. Maybe it was the diesel exhaust he enjoyed more. The smell of his work. His first love.

The smell of freedom. Sure as heck didn't smell diesel exhaust in the pen.

Didn't smell exotic flowers, either.

He shrugged that thought off along with its companion: diesel exhaust represented his *second* love.

Sighing, he opened his eyes. An underwear model, her skin golden and glistening, her lips pursed in a seductive, beckoning pout, stared down at him from the billboard on top of the rise. Her glossy hair covered one high cheekbone, but he still recognized her.

Cassidy.

The entire billboard was in neutral colors, except for her blue eyes and the tiny, tiny blue bra and underwear set she wore.

His breath caught in his throat, and his chest hurt. He'd wondered occasionally if she looked as good under those soft blue jeans and loose sweaters as he figured she must. He'd seen a picture or two of her at high school dances back in the day. He'd heard she competed in beauty pageants and did some modeling, but other than the Homecoming picture on the front page of the paper, he'd never seen that side of her. He swallowed, unable to look away from the billboard. Not yet.

That picture right there was better than any pinups he'd seen. Better than the occasional picture the guards sometimes passed around, illegally, of course. And Torque had never much been interested. Now he wondered if Cassidy had been in any of the pics that had exchanged hands on the inside, and he wasn't sure how he felt about all those eyes on her body. Not that he had any say. It wasn't his. *She* wasn't his.

He couldn't keep the disappointment from eating up his inside. He supposed modeling was a career that paid well and some women sought, but Cassidy had so much potential for more. Maybe he'd hoped that she'd made something out of her life while he was locked up. None of his business.

Taking another deep breath, he ripped his eyes away from the billboard.

He was just setting the third triangle out along the highway where the cars were barely slowing down as they flashed past when the flashing lights pulled along the road. He straightened, face-to-face with the Pennsylvania law as a free man for the first time in ten years.

Swallowing the anxiety that bubbled like battery acid up his throat, he strode as casually as he could to the patrol car and met the officer there.

She was short and curvy, with her patrolman's hat tilting over her dark brown eyes set in flawless olive skin. She wasn't smiling. He'd never learned to flirt, and since the current time didn't seem like the most optimal time to begin self-instruction, he returned her look with a non-smiling one of his own. Figuring it was her prerogative to speak first, he held his hands where she could see them and waited. If there was one thing he'd gotten good at after ten years in the slammer, it was waiting.

"You the driver?" She jerked her head at the bus.

"No."

She had her mouth open to ask another question, but it closed at his unexpected answer. Her lips pursed together, and she raised her brows.

He wasn't compliant by nature, and she'd had her chance to take control of the situation. "Driver's an old guy. I volunteered to set the flares up. If you've got a pair of vice grips..."

He waited for her to answer his implied question, but her face remained blank. She didn't know what vice grips were.

"I'll pinch off the airline so we can move the bus off the road."

"It can move?" A little chink in her face armor appeared as she glanced at the bus, then her eyes swiftly ran across his torso before meeting his gaze again.

Stinking t-shirt was too tight. He'd never thought to have his brothers bring him something bigger to wear home. "Not unless we get the airline pinched off."

She regained control of her face. "If we can get it down to the exit, that'd be better than sitting here along the road. I'm going to have to shut a lane down."

"You have a box of tools or anything in your cruiser?"

She tilted her head. "There's something under the seat. Let me look." She turned then stopped and looked back. "Um, what do they look like?"

In the end, she brought the whole box out to him and set it on the hood. He fingered through the sparse number of tools, remembering just in time not to let his fingers linger and caress the cool smooth metal. Having his fingers on those tools was more like coming home than actually walking into his gram's trailer.

The lady trooper gave him an odd look, and he focused his wandering thoughts. First thing he was going to buy with his first paycheck was a set of tools, the best he could afford. He could fondle a wrench in his hand all day long if he wanted and sleep with a ratchet and socket set under his pillow. Not now.

He took a last look at the set in front of him. No vice grips. He pulled out the zip ties. These would work if...

"You got a blade on you?" Since he'd been about five, he'd carried a pocketknife on him everywhere he went. They'd taken it when he was arrested and never given it back. That was next on his list of things to buy after the tool set.

"No."

Surely someone on the bus had a pocketknife. "Gimme about ten minutes, and I'll have it fixed up good enough to limp her down to the exit."

She nodded, her face relaxing a little. "There's a big truck stop right at the end of the exit ramp. Do you think it could make it that far?"

"Yeah. No problem."

"Okay. Let me know when you're ready to pull out, and I'll follow with my lights on."

"'Preciate it." Torque strode back to the bus and poked his head in the door. "You have a knife on you? I'll need to cut the line."

The driver shook his head.

"Mind if I ask if anyone has one?"

"Help yourself."

Torque stepped up and called out over the low murmur of voices, "Anyone have a blade I can borrow to fix the bus?"

No one said anything for a few moments. Then a big-shouldered, tough-looking dude at the back called out, "I've got one. Come get it."

Torque walked back the narrow aisle toward the man who spoke. If they weren't on a cheap bus bound for nowhere, Torque might have thought that as big as he was the dude was a professional football player. But the hard look in the guy's eyes was as familiar as his own breath.

He stopped at his seat.

The guy stared at him hard for a minute, sizing him up. Torque kept his gaze steady and his face impassive. He'd never bulked up like some guys had, although his shoulders had widened. But he didn't cower or even feel fear. He'd learned that it wasn't normally the big guys that one needed to watch out for.

A small movement of the guy's brow broke the stare. A shadow of a smile touched his lip before he flicked his ten-inch knife out of the boot that rested across his knee. He flipped it around, his fingers graceful and sure, before offering it to Torque, handle first.

Torque stared at his wrist and the "M" with the flying rat tattoo. Mexican Mafia. Ruthless. Vicious. Pitiless. Yeah. He knew it from experience.

His poker face had become his greatest asset in prison, but he'd stared at the tattoo an instant too long. His eyes flicked back up to the man's face where a smirk slouched on his mouth. The three tattooed dots by his right eye, representing the gang lifestyle, crinkled together as his eyes narrowed.

God forbid the dude think Torque was somehow an enemy. "Thanks, bro." He gripped the handle. Intricately carved, it felt smooth and warm in his hand. "I'll take care of it and make sure you get it back."

The guy jerked his head. Torque broke the number one unwritten rule from his time inside and turned his back on a man he didn't trust, walking back to the front of the bus and back out into the glorious bright air of freedom. Maybe he'd pitch a tent in his gram's backyard and live outside for the rest of his life.

It took a few minutes to figure out how to get the skirting off the bus, and a few more to weasel his way under it enough to reach the airline that needed to be severed and wire-tied off. He made his ten-minute deadline, though, and the patrolwoman pulled out behind the bus, lights flashing.

After delivering the knife back to the Mexican Mafia dude, Torque returned to his seat and sunk down into the cloth cradle. Felt good to be useful again. To have something to occupy his hands and to have honest work to accomplish. Wish he had a job lined up.

His brother Tough had a body shop and did some light mechanical work on small cars. Torque was good enough with his hands that he could be a help to Tough. But it was the big trucks and the diesel motors that was in his blood. That's where his heart was and where he wanted to be. It had been his dream forever to own his own diesel repair shop. To feel the power and vibrations, to breathe the exhaust, to work in the grease.

But he'd take what he could get, he supposed, since he'd be starting from the ground up. His brothers had told him that the shop he'd worked in as a kid had closed down after old man Miller had passed away. Made his heart feel a little painful pinch thinking about the kind old man who'd taken him in as a grade school kid and given him a few bucks a week to sweep the shop and wash trucks. His responsibilities had increased over the years until he'd been the main mechanic and the main money-earner for the shop as he tore down the mechanical motors and rebuilt them.

But old man Miller was gone, his shop closed down. Turbo had told him that much on one of his visits.

He leaned his head back against the headrest and closed his eyes. Wasn't going to worry about tomorrow.

"Hey, sonny."

Turning his head, he opened his eyes. The little old lady beside him peered at him from over the top of her thick glasses.

He blinked. She must have been talking to him, but he was one hundred percent sure he didn't know her.

"Yeah?"

"You're the Baxter boy. The one that went to prison." She put her hand on his arm.

His body wanted to flinch, and he fought the urge to hide. Stupid side effects of freaking prison.

"Yeah."

"I remember my husband talking about you. Remember him showing me your picture in the newspaper." She grinned, and somehow, even with the wrinkled skin, smart but sunken blue eyes, and wild, white hair, she looked youthful. Girly.

He'd won the local fair's pulling contest the summer before he went up. He was only sixteen and had built the motor himself. Paper made a big deal about it, and he'd landed on the front page. Not that he had parents to give a crap, although Gram had seemed pretty proud of it since she cut the article out and used one of her Christmas magnets to stick it on the refrigerator.

The lady didn't seem to need him to talk, so he didn't.

She leaned closer. "He was jealous of that old man Miller. Said with a kid like you working in the shop, the sly old fellow would never lack customers."

He shrugged. The bus slowed as it came to the end of the exit ramp. It wasn't hard to see the big truck stop just ahead to the right. Looked like his patch job was gonna hold.

The lady tightened her fingers on his arm. He focused back on her face. "You weren't visiting that prison. You were leaving it."

"Yeah."

"My Tyke could always fix anything and wasn't afraid to stand up and say so." She let go of his arm and placed both hands on the purse on her lap. "Do you have a job lined up?"

He hesitated before answering, just because he wasn't sure what to say. That was the one question she could have asked that would make him curious. "Kinda."

"If it doesn't work out, I'd like to talk to you. Tyke's Garage. Take Seventh Street out of town in the opposite direction of Miller's, and it's at the top of the hill overlooking Brickly Springs."

Now he knew who she was and where she was talking about. "You were in the sewing circle with my gram." The year his mother died, Gram's sewing circle had made him and his brothers each a new quilt. His oldest brother, Ben, fourteen at the time, had taken off after the quilt but before the funeral. Hadn't heard from him since. His dad left a couple years before and didn't bother coming back for the funeral, let alone birthdays or Christmas. But Tough and Turbo, in third and first grades, if he remembered correctly, since he'd been in fourth grade and they were one and three years younger, had stayed. As he had. They were too little to do anything else. Too little to put the pieces of their broken family back together, too, although Gram had tried. The quilting group had helped.

He refocused on the lady beside him. "I'm sorry. I didn't recognize you."

"It's been a good many years." She pressed her lips together. "I was over in Philly at the doctor's. Been going for years. Ever since I had the cancer."

He couldn't believe she went to her appointment alone. "Where are your daughters?" If he remembered correctly, she had two.

"They both work. It's not like I'm too old to find my way around myself. This was just the regular checkup." She gripped her purse with both hands but seemed to relax a little as they talked.

"Grandkids?" he asked after a moment. It was odd to have a fairly normal conversation.

"Nope. Both my girls were modern women who didn't want kids."

The bus jerked to a stop at the far side of the truck stop. Torque barely noticed. He supposed he couldn't judge, since his mother, if she were alive, would hardly be proud of where he'd been, but he thought maybe she'd be a little pleased at the circumstances that had landed him there and the stand he'd taken. But, if his mother were alive, he'd be treating her like a queen, not making her take the bus to a doctor's appointment in Philly.

Maybe one had to lose their mother to really appreciate her. 'Course, he couldn't say the same about his dad, so maybe that's where his personality flaw was. He just differentiated between leaving on purpose and leaving with no choice. Cancer hadn't cared that his mom had four boys who needed her.

He looked again at the old lady beside him. She'd been a friend to his gram through the loss of her daughter. She and her friends had done all they knew to do to comfort four grieving boys after the death of their mother.

It wasn't that he owed her anything, but he wanted to feel like a human again. Doing something nice for someone without thought of repayment. Taking care of someone other than himself. Man, even just looking at a sweet, little old lady, made him feel like he was alive and in the world of the living again. Color and softness. Tools that fit in his hand. Boots that made him feel like a man again. Jeans and soon a t-shirt that actually fit.

She'd asked him to go talk to her, and he would. "I need to see my gram. Might not make it out today, but I'll walk up tomorrow."

The lady nodded and settled her purse in her lap. "I'll expect you around lunchtime. Come hungry."

He wasn't sure exactly what she was offering, but it wouldn't hurt to check it out.

Chapter 3

"What he'd say? How'd it go? How did he look?" Kelly Williams fired question after question at Cassidy as she stepped through her apartment door. Cassidy sighed and leaned against the closed door. Kelly was a bundle of energy, and sometimes it was almost overwhelming.

"I'm sorry. I'm doing it again, aren't I?" Kelly asked ruefully. Her ponytail swung as she bounced one of the twins Cassidy was fostering with the hope of adopting on her hip.

"Mom!" Jamal, the twins' older brother, whom Cassidy had already adopted, came running out.

"How was school today?" she asked.

He gave the requisite "good" and mumbled something about a paper in his backpack. She handed him an apple, and he raced back into the living room where he was putting a model airplane together on the high table where the twins couldn't reach it.

Cassidy shook her head and pushed off from the door. "No. It's not you." Nissa held her little arms out, and Cassidy threw her purse down before taking her from Kelly. As the little arms encircled her neck, she sighed inside. Was there anything sweeter than the love of an innocent child?

"I'm thinking it didn't go well."

"No." With the typical three-second attention span of a twelve-month-old, Nissa straightened her legs and shifted her body. Cassidy set her down and watched her toddle to the living room and join her sister on the floor with the blocks scattered everywhere.

"He hates me, and he doesn't want to have anything to do with me."

Kelly gasped. "Did he tell you that?"

"Not exactly." She turned to the counter and started wiping without really paying attention. "But he took the bus rather than ride home with me, and I had to practically beg him to come to the sponsor meeting tomorrow night." She was getting tired of begging. She'd begged every official she knew to pass the legislative permission required to start and fund the sponsorship for prisoners program. Now, Torque, the whole reason she fought for the program to begin with, didn't even want to be part of it.

"Not good." Kelly moved around the kitchen, as familiar with Cassidy's as with her own, and began making tea.

Cassidy forced a smile, hoping to cover her acute discouragement. "You treat me better than I deserve."

"That's what friends are for. You'd do the same for me."

A knock sounded on the door. "That's probably Harris." Harris would have hurried over as soon as she closed the library for the day. "Better set another cup out."

Kelly was already on it, while Cassidy went and opened her door.

Harris only needed one look at her face. "Not good, huh?" She walked in and wrapped her arms around Cassidy.

Cassidy hugged her back. "It's that obvious?"

"I'm afraid so."

They sat down at the table where Cassidy could keep an eye on the twins and Jamal. She smiled at his concentration as he carefully separated the parts of the airplane. At eight years old, he was four years younger than the recommended age on the airplane box, but this was the third one he'd put together. Her son had a gift.

"He didn't want to come home with me. He didn't want to do the sponsorship program. Basically, he hates my guts."

"He didn't say that," Kelly reminded her.

Like he had needed to.

"So he's not doing the sponsorship program?" Harris asked, her brows drawn, her expression concerned. She knew how hard and for how many years Cassidy had fought for that program.

"He said he'd come to the meeting tomorrow night. He didn't commit."

"You're still in love with him," Kelly, direct as always, stated over the rim of her tea cup.

"I was never 'in love' with him. Infatuated maybe." He was the first person in her life who seemed to see beyond the good looks she'd been born with to the brain that lay under it. He's the one who said she should be a doctor. When she told him she couldn't stand the sight of blood, he'd said, "Well, a lawyer, then." And that's what she'd done. She'd still earned some money as an underwear model, and that helped put her through law school. Her parents, the owners of a vast empire of various kinds of pickles, now semi-retired, would have paid. But with Torque in prison, serving her time, she hadn't been able to live the high life. It wouldn't have been right.

Harris and Kelly just looked at her. They didn't believe that she'd never been in love with Torque.

"Really." The best memories of her life were riding beside him. Her last carefree days. Maybe that's why she cherished them so much. "I just..." She spread her hands out on the table. Even her friends didn't know about that night and what happened and what exactly Torque had done. She hadn't even known Kelly then. And she hadn't become friends with either Harris or Kelly until a couple of years ago when she graduated from law school and became a public defender in her hometown.

"Wasn't he your boyfriend in high school?"

"No."

Her friends had accepted her explanation about feeling bad for Torque because he had been given an unfair, too harsh sentence. She hadn't realized that they both, apparently, thought she had feelings for him.

"Never?" Harris asked gently.

"No. We didn't even go to the same school." At least not from her second grade year on, when the private, all-girls' school had opened in the next town over. Torque would have been in Kindergarten.

"You're older than him."

"Yes." Which she figured was why he'd done what he did. She was nineteen, a sophomore at Stanford, but home from college to attend the homecoming football game and give it some publicity. She'd never been a superstar model, but she'd been well enough known that the homecoming committee had requested her presence.

He was only seventeen, a senior in high school. But Torque always seemed older. Maybe because of his hard life. Or because he was quiet. Serious.

Still, she had assumed, and he probably had too, that they'd not charge a seventeen-year-old as an adult. She'd been wrong.

Her tea was getting cold. She picked the cup up, surprised to see her hands trembling.

"If he agreed to come to the meeting, maybe he'll agree to do the program," Harris said reasonably.

Cassidy hoped so. Not only would it look good on his record, and not only would it help her save face, since it would be embarrassing to have fought so long and so hard for it only to have her first sponsor ditch her, but it was a way for her to help him. Maybe.

Cassidy changed the subject to Kelly's latest charity project, and they talked a little about the activity center she was hoping to start, which both Harris and Cassidy had agreed to help with.

"How's the adoption coming?" Kelly asked as they stood, clearing off the table and putting their cups in the dishwasher.

"I meet with my caseworker the day after tomorrow. It's been six weeks since their mom was sent to prison, and they finally got the dad, who's in for life, to sign off on custody."

"Did they decide that you were okay as a single mother?"

"No. They're very firm that I could adopt one child as a single mother, but their policy is firm that they don't allow a single mother to have two children under the age of three by herself." She sighed, looking over at the twins, who now had every doll and stuffed animal they owned scattered out on the floor with the blocks. "I, uh." She paused. "I might have told them that I'm seeing someone and it's serious."

"I didn't know you were seeing someone. Let alone that it was serious." Harris's slightly cultured voice held a tone of complete disbelief.

"I'm not."

Kelly rolled her eyes. "Is that what they're coming for tomorrow? To meet him?"

"No, I told them we weren't living together. They agreed to let me foster the twins. Only because they really like to keep siblings together. So, that's what they're coming to see, that I'm doing okay with Jamal and the twins in a foster situation. They might allow me to keep them longer—until my nonexistent serious boyfriend proposes or moves in—if things look good to them."

"Where are you finding a serious boyfriend?"

"I hope that they'll decide I'm doing well and that they'll make an exception this time." She leaned against the counter. "I know it was wrong to lie. I actually didn't mean to. Didn't really think about it. But when she explained her policy, we were sitting in the conference room. Jamal was playing with his sisters, and he was so happy. He wanted to be with his siblings so desperately. It's all he has, and he feels protective of them. I had to do everything in my power to keep them together." She ran her finger along the edge of the counter. "The words slipped out, and I thought it would give me the time I needed to form a plan."

"They haven't asked to meet him yet?"

"They said eventually he'll have to fill out papers, but since he's not living with me and we're not engaged, they'd wait." She gave a little smile. "Maybe they didn't want me to scare him off."

"Can't scare him off if you don't have him."

"He doesn't exist."

Cassidy shook her head, her chest feeling like curdled milk swished around in it. This was the second big lie in her life. The first was allowing Torque to serve her time. Technically she'd never lied about that, but she'd allowed him to.

Harris glanced at her watch. "Oh wow. It's late. I have a meeting at the hospital about helping install a children's library in the new wing of the hospital." She slipped her sweater back on and headed for the door. "I gave you a good recommendation. If they need something more, I'll do whatever I can."

Cassidy hugged her. "I know. Thanks so much. Those little girls have stolen my heart, and Jamal is such a proud big brother. He's so happy to have them here."

Kelly came over and gave Cassidy a hug as well. "I have to head down to the children's center and help serve dinner. Call me if you need me."

"I will. Thanks so much."

Cassidy shut the door behind them. As if on cue, one of the twins started screaming. The second one joined in. As she hurried to them, she wondered if she really was maybe biting off too much for a single woman. But Jamal needed to grow up with his sisters, and they deserved to know their big brother.

Dodging the blocks, a baby doll with a broken arm, and several other brightly colored noisemakers, she sat on the floor and pulled each crying twin onto her lap.

Tomorrow, she'd be back at the office, and they'd be at day care. Maybe they deserved a mother who would stay home with them. Or a family where they'd have both a mom and a dad. That seemed to be her life now, trying to figure out what was best for her children, for the defendants on her docket, and for the inmates she had been fighting for.

Everything her life consisted of now, aside from the residual ads that she'd shot last year and were still running, had been born of that night when Torque had shoved her flip phone and purse at her and told her to leave. She couldn't waste a life that had been bought with such a sacrifice. Keeping this little family together—Jamal and his sisters—was just one more thing in the long list of things that she'd tried to do to make her life count. To say thank you.

Maybe that was thanks enough, since after seeing him today, it was obvious he didn't want anything else from her.

Chapter 4

Torque climbed the steps to his gram's trailer. Everything seemed a little more worn, tired. Or maybe that was just him. Worn and tired.

He thought he'd be jubilant on his first day of freedom, but maybe the stress or excitement had been too much and worn him out. Whatever it was, he climbed the steps wearily, giving two short raps on the door before walking in. The scent of roast beef mingled with the unique scent of Gram's home, one thing that hadn't changed at all in the time he'd been gone.

Turbo and Tough sat at the small kitchen table with Gram looking even smaller and more frail than she had when she'd visited him in prison.

His brothers got up and walked over, hugging him and slapping him on the back. Torque felt the oddest urge to cry—an urge he couldn't remember feeling since the day his mother's casket went in the ground. That day, too, he'd hugged his brothers and fought tears. He'd determined to be the best big brother ever, since his little brothers didn't have a mother or a dad. It was also the last thing he'd ever said to his mother, since her dying words to him had extracted his promise to take care of them. As sincere as an eleven-year-old could ever be, he'd looked his mother in her beautiful sea-green eyes and said, "I promise I'll be the best big brother ever."

He'd been determined to keep that promise.

Then a pair of seductive blue eyes had slanted a few looks at him, and his promise had flown out the window, disappearing like exhaust fumes on a windy day. He'd sacrificed the last years of his brothers' high school and the all-important first few years of new adulthood on the altar of being a playgirl's prince charming.

Man, he was a stupid little snit when he was seventeen.

"Where's your escort?" Turbo gave him one last slap then bent down to look out the window. "Didn't hear her pull in."

"Her?" Tough asked, his brows drawn down over the same brown eyes that all three brothers shared.

"Cassidy Kimball. She called me a few weeks ago and mumbled something about a sponsor program and asked if she could pick you up." Turbo gave a crooked grin. He'd always smiled more than anyone else Torque knew, and his laughing eyes hadn't changed much. Maybe just a little older. Maybe there was a little wisdom lurking in their depths now. "I've seen her picture on the billboards on the interstate. Figured it wouldn't be a hardship to ride beside her for three hours."

"Get out of the way and let an old lady hug her grandson." Gram pushed Tough and Turbo aside. Torque didn't remember her using a cane before. He squeezed her gently, her small figure so much more frail than he'd remembered. A part of him wanted to be bitter at the wasted years, and he had to swat that part away. He had no one but himself to blame. Cassidy shouldn't have gotten in his truck, but he'd been the fool who had jumped in after her, and he'd been the even bigger fool who had taken the blame for what happened next.

He squeezed Gram a little harder. A shaft of nerves pinched in his stomach. "Where's Mrs. Conrad?" The widow of the man his pickup had killed that night.

Gram's hand patted his back. "She's fine. Your brothers and that fancy woman been looking after her."

He didn't ask who the fancy woman was. There was a more important question. "She willing to see me, you think?"

"Land's sake. She sure is. She was broken up about losing her husband for a while, of course she was. But accidents happen, and she's a God-fearing woman. Forgiveness came to her eventually."

His stomach unwound, and he released the breath he didn't realize he was holding. "That's good. I need to apologize."

"She'll hear it, son. And she'll forgive you. She wanted to see you in prison, but I told her that tweren't no place for the likes of her."

"She's a fancy lady?" Torque asked with a little tilt of his lips, imitating Gram's last statement.

"You get yourself rid of that smart mouth, young man. You mighta got away with that in prison, but there'll be no smartin' off here."

Over Gram's head, Turbo mimed her and then bit his thumb at Torque, a gesture that was at once as familiar as breathing, yet felt like a million years ago that they'd borrowed the gesture from Shakespeare, and Torque's eleventh grade English class, and used it among themselves, since using the normal certain single finger gesture would get their mouths washed out with soap, never mind their mouths hadn't said anything.

Torque couldn't stay serious in the face of Turbo's grin, which was pretty much the typical reaction of anyone around Turbo, and he bit his own thumb in response.

Tough, not to be left out, and never one to waste words when a gesture would do, bit his thumb as well.

Gram didn't even look at them. "I know exactly what that means, and none of you are too big to bend your head over my kitchen sink. I'll expect you all to keep a civil tongue in your heads. Or else."

Gosh, it was good to be home.

THE NEXT AFTERNOON followed an especially stressful day at work in which Cassidy questioned her decision to become a public defender. Why hadn't she chosen the starvation mixed with endless exercise, constant cutthroat competition, backbiting, and relative uncertainty of even getting a paycheck by pursuing a modeling career?

Which, she had to say, juggling one crabby twin in one arm and trying to appease the other who was seated in the shopping cart, seemed like child's play to the life and work she currently had. At least today.

She pushed the cart past the candy aisle and called to Jamal, "This way, hon."

"But you promised me candy if I got an A on my book report and poster."

She was the most horrible mother in the world, because she had, indeed, promised him candy. "Did you get it back?"

"Today. It's in my book bag."

If she didn't give him what she promised, she'd be even worse than the most horrible mother in the world, but there was not a single cell in her body that wanted the fight, whining, and potential meltdown and fit that would ensue if she took her tired, crabby, hungry twins down that aisle. She'd been trying so hard to get them all to eat better. She didn't have to be model thin anymore, but she didn't want her kids to die of heart attacks in elementary school, either. The adoption agency would probably have an opinion on that.

It was on the tip of her tongue to ask him to wait until another day, but she couldn't get the words past her lips after seeing the hopeful, eager, proud look on Jamal's face. He'd worked hard on that project, despite his frustration with reading the book that was slightly above his level.

Nessa, in her arms, yanked at a handful of her hair. It slipped from the no-nonsense bun she'd piled it into before dawn this morning. After a few more good yanks, Nessa dropped the hair and started to fight Nissa for the necklace Cassidy had forgotten to remove after work.

Nessa poked Nissa in the eye. Nissa started crying and scratched Nessa. Then, in less than a microsecond flat, they were both screaming at the top of their lungs. Nessa wanted down and Nissa wanted up, and Jamal still stood there in the candy aisle, looking for all the world like a lost puppy begging for one tiny little scrap of food to fill his aching tummy.

"Yes," Cassidy said.

Jamal tilted his head. He mouthed a word that Cassidy couldn't hear over the screaming of the twins. She read his lips. "What?"

"Yes," she said in as quiet a scream as she could and still be heard over the twins. She continued in the same tone, "Pick it out and meet me in the vegetable section." She would atone for the little bit of candy by buying more fresh vegetables that she would be too tired to cook when she got home.

Thankful for her small-town grocery store—she would never leave her eight-year-old alone in a big-city supercenter—she tried to give both twins what they wanted as she used her hip and the occasional knee to push her shopping cart toward the fresh vegetables. She could shop for healthy stuff for the rest of the week and buy just one frozen pizza for supper tonight.

One clerk gave her a pitying look. The next one she passed, a younger version of herself, gave a judgmental frown at the noise her children were making. Or maybe she heard Cassidy tell her eight-year-old to pick his own candy out. Whatever. She'd looked at parents the same way before she had children. It was harder than it looked, and if the twins weren't screaming so loud, she might have told the girl that.

At least the store wasn't too busy. Cassidy was able to fly along, grabbing carrots, spinach, and several zucchini and throwing them in the cart. There was an older gentleman standing in front of the potatoes that she was able to squeeze by while snagging a five-pound bag, and a tall, broad-shouldered man wearing a ball cap who stood in front of the mushrooms. Jamal loved mushrooms, and she wasn't leaving the store without them. One would think the guy would hear the kids screaming and at least hurry his selection, but no, he stood there with one hand in his pocket like he had all day to decide on sliced or whole. Like it even really freaking mattered.

Cassidy bent and picked up Nessa's sippy cup for the eighth time. Even though grocery stores had to be filthy germ pits, she'd quit wiping it off on her dry-clean-only skirt after the third time. Nessa batted it away. Cassidy lost her grip, and the cup flew over, smacking Nissa on the head. Her screams ratcheted up, and she jerked her little body around, flinging her own sippy cup.

It was one of those slow-motion things where Cassidy watched the cup tumble through the air. Even before it hit the man just below his ear, Cassidy realized who it was. The hit. Like thunder, the *thunk* came after. He turned. No surprise in his eyes.

A million thoughts flew through her head, but the one that made the most impact was *he knew it was me and he was ignoring me.*

He truly did hate her.

With the horrible day she'd had, with her one client being one of those who was guilty as sin, and she had to force herself to defend him, the judge moving the trial date to accommodate his hemorrhoid surgery, and her coworker quitting, dumping her workload onto Cassidy, then with twins missing their naps and there being no food in her house, on top of the candy issue and her acute insecurity about her even being fit to be a mother to a used doll baby, let alone real, live children, somehow, Torque's hate on top of everything made her stupid, traitorous eyes water.

But she would show up in court naked with bunny ears strapped to her head before she cried in front of this man.

She shoved the cart with her hip, eyeing the sippy cup that had landed between Torque's boots. "I'm sorry," she yelled, keeping her head lowered as she swooped down to retrieve the cup, planning to grab it, grab her other twin and Jamal, and drive half an hour to Altoona to the closest McDonald's drive-thru. At least if she ate the fast food with them, they could all die of a heart attack together.

But she hadn't anticipated him bending down to get the cup, hadn't thought she'd end up frozen, six inches from his serious brown eyes, hadn't counted on the powerful attraction she always felt in his presence being amplified with two toddlers screaming in her ears.

She couldn't move. Her heart thudded in her throat. Her breath came in small gasps. The world was still turning, the twins still crying, and life went on. For everyone but her.

Her neck grew warm, and her arm trembled with the awkward way she held Nessa, but she couldn't cut her gaze from his.

He looked away first. His eyes fell to her lips. Which were suddenly dry, and she licked them. Something hot flared in his gaze, before his eyes shuttered completely. He straightened, holding the cup.

Feeling as graceful as a pregnant elephant, Cassidy managed to get upright with Nessa still on her hip, despite her shaking legs and heart.

"Give me your list. I'll do your shopping. You can take them home." His deep voice cut through the twins crying. As if by magic, they both stopped, and with puffy little breaths and wet cheeks, they stared at the dark stranger.

"I couldn't ask you to do that."

One brow raised. "It would be a mercy for the other shoppers in the store."

No doubt.

"Consider it your good deed for the day."

Anger flared before she realized his eyes held what could be considered a twinkle.

She grabbed the diaper bag and pulled her keys from her purse. "It's on a blue sheet of paper. There's cash in my wallet, and my address is on my driver's license."

"You're leaving your purse with me?"

"Yes." After all, if he skipped town and drained every cent in her accounts, it still wouldn't be as much as she owed him. She glanced at her purse, stamped with multicolored flowers on an off-white background. She'd bought it from the local discount store specifically because it looked like it would hide a multitude of dirt and was big enough to double as a diaper bag if the need arose. "Problem with it?"

Lifting one broad shoulder, he said, "It doesn't really go with my outfit, and I think it'll make my butt look big."

He didn't crack a smile. His eyes barely flickered. She'd forgotten how much she loved his droll humor.

She smiled, feeling some of her tiredness, if not her hurt, drain away.

"Hey, Mom. Who's he?"

Cassidy turned. Jamal staggered toward her carrying the biggest bag of candy she'd ever seen. It must have weighed ten pounds. So that's what had taken him so long. True to his nature, he'd studied every box and bag in the candy aisle and picked out the biggest. Lesson learned. Next time, she'd have to be more specific. One *piece* of candy.

"This is Mr. Baxter." Like a coordinated event, the twins started crying together. Cassidy raised her voice to be heard over them. "He's going to finish our grocery shopping. Put the candy in the cart and come with me." She glanced at Torque. Any good nature had disappeared from his eyes. His face was a closed, unreadable mask. "Is that still okay?"

He shrugged. Her attention was caught again by the width of his shoulders, but the nagging thought that he was irritated with her somehow wouldn't leave.

She wasn't going to turn down help. "Come on, Jamal."

Chapter 5

Torque watched her walk away. Slender and tall like she'd always been. The top of her head came to his nose. She fit perfectly in his arms.

He glanced again at the purse she'd so casually left behind, then at her retreating back, a baby on each hip and the little boy following her. The kid was eight maybe? Nine? He'd only been in prison a year or two before she was off with another man.

Cassidy and Torque, they'd never been exclusive. Never even dated, really. But he'd never been with another woman. Hadn't been interested.

He turned to her purse and gingerly picked it up. Apparently, she'd gotten over him pretty quickly. Or hadn't been that into him to begin with, which was what he'd figured out in prison. He was just her man-toy. Or some kind of plaything that she trifled with when all of her other boyfriends were busy.

He'd known it, but it still hurt to have it shoved in his face when that little boy called her "mom."

Opening the purse wider, he searched without touching anything for the blue list. Wonder what Mr. Cassidy would say about Torque riffling through his wife's purse. The man had better not be home. If he were there, sitting on the couch with his feet propped up while Cassidy struggled through the grocery store still dressed in her work clothes and juggling two screaming babies and trailing a nine-year-old with the instincts of a street rat—Torque eyed the ten-pound bag of candy—then it wouldn't be hard to want to use a few of the moves he'd learned in prison to teach the man a thing or two about taking care of his wife.

He spied the blue piece of paper poking out from under her wallet. It galled him, but he'd have to use her money to buy her groceries. After the bus ticket, he had exactly eleven dollars and thirty-two cents to his name. Gram had given him forty bucks and a short list. He hated it, but he'd taken the money from her too. The last time, he swore.

Earlier, he'd visited Mrs. Conrad and apologized, which had been an emotional experience for both of them. She'd been so loving and forgiving, he'd felt ashamed of his petty issues with Cassidy. He'd lost ten years, sure, but he hadn't lost his life or the lives of anyone close to him. Yet, Mrs. Conrad hadn't seemed bitter or angry or vengeful. He only hoped he could be like her someday.

After that, he'd gone to the library, been schooled on how to use the internet to apply for jobs, and put his application in various places. He'd even walked to an onsite interview at the local hardware store which was having open interviews all day.

He had to be honest about serving time—the question had been on all his applications. Tomorrow, he was visiting Mrs. Ford, the lady from the bus, then starting work for Tough until one of the other places called. He needed a cell phone. Apparently everyone had them now.

It didn't take long to finish shopping. He dug her driver's license out and stopped short when he read the address. Cassidy's place wasn't that far from where his gram lived—about a ten-minute walk. It surprised him, to be honest.

There were boarded-up houses and grass growing out of the cracks in the sidewalks. Bricks crumbled from the corner of the apartment building she lived in. There were very few streetlights, and it was dark as he shifted the six bags of groceries and pulled open the door to the apartments. It wasn't even locked.

What kind of man had she married?

Why was she living in a place like this when her picture was splashed all over billboards across the state? He'd seen at least three after he'd noticed the first one on the way home.

Not to mention there was the fortune that her family had.

There were definitely some things here that weren't adding up. He climbed up a second flight of steps, turned right down a dark hall, and stopped in front of apartment #306.

Using his elbow, he knocked on her door. Frustration balled up inside him. This place was a hellhole, and he couldn't even tell her about it. He didn't have the money nor the right to move her out.

He was about ready to knock again when the door opened. Cassidy stood in the door, still in her fancy blouse and skirt, her hair no longer hanging in her face but pulled severely back into a bun. Tiredness pinched her features, but she had her game face on.

"Come in."

She held out her hands like she was going to take the bags from him, but he ignored her and set them on the counter. They were all hers since he'd pocketed his gram's list. To get both would have been more than he could carry.

"I appreciate it. Let me pay you for your time."

"No." He bit his tongue on what he wanted her to do with her money.

She crossed her arms and leaned a hip against the counter. The scent of exotic flowers wafted in the air. It pulled every good memory from the recesses of his mind. He almost groaned under the onslaught.

"I really do appreciate this. I'm not sure if I would have made it through. Thankfully, I had four eggs in the fridge. One for each twin, and Jamal ate two."

"You haven't eaten?" She needed to eat. The woman was barely staying upright from exhaustion and hunger, too, probably.

"No, and unless you picked up a frozen pizza, which was not on my list, I'm not going to. I'm way too tired to cook."

He hadn't picked up a pizza, never even thought about getting anything that wasn't on her list. He looked around the small apartment, noticing for the first time that it was dim and quiet. "You here by yourself?"

Her brows furrowed, like his very reasonable question confused her, but she shook her head. "The kids are in bed. There was some kind of special thing at the day care today, and the twins missed their nap. They were as tired as me."

"I'll stay here. Go get yourself something to eat."

She sighed. "Too tired."

"Gimme your keys. I'll get something." Eleven bucks would buy her a salad at the gas station up the road.

"You haven't gotten your license back yet."

Of course not. He'd woken up in a prison cell yesterday morning. For the last time in his life, hopefully. He held his hand out. "You go, or I'm going for you."

She walked around the counter and grabbed her keys off the wall. "I'd like a grilled chicken salad, a fruit and yogurt cup, and a coffee, black, from the Herald's Gas Station. I'll leave the door open, and you can just throw it on the counter."

"Keep your door locked. I assume your house key is on this ring." He held up her keys, and she nodded. "I can unlock the door. I'll set the keys and the food on the counter. No coffee. It's too late to be drinking that stuff."

"I have three briefs to look over and a trial to prepare for tomorrow. If you don't get the coffee, I'll brew my own."

What briefs? Like underwear? Did she pick the kind she was going to model? A trial? What was she on trial for?

He opened his mouth to ask, but she seemed to sway a little, and he noticed anew the dark circles under her eyes. "Go lie down. I'll be back in ten with some food." Man, he'd like to strangle her husband. He must be a construction worker or truck driver, or maybe he worked the night shift at the paper mill.

"I'm going to put these groceries away first."

"It won't hurt anything in there to sit out for another ten minutes. Get your butt over to that couch and lie down before you fall down."

Her eyes flashed, and she took a step toward him, raising a finger. Something inside of him rose up, pressing him forward to meet her, grabbing her hand, but not in a power grip. His fingers closed gently, forming more of a tender cradle, holding her hand the way he wanted to hold her.

"I know," he said in a softer, gentler tone, which mimicked the care of his hand. "I'm a jerk because I tell you what to do. Haven't forgotten you might have mentioned that a time or two, way back when." His heart squeezed at the memories. Her eyes closed. He swallowed.

Her breath blew over his face. It smelled like the soul of the woman he loved. Like hot nights and cold water. Summer sunsets and midnight air. A country song on his radio and the rumble of the truck he'd build from the rails up. Of silky hair blowing across his face and a slender body pressed to his.

Kiss her.

She wasn't his. She was never his.

"Cassidy," he breathed around the excruciating ache in his chest. "Please lie down."

Her mouth trembled then tightened. Her hand fisted in his. He thought she was going to fight, and he almost welcomed it. There was so much unfinished between them. But she yanked away and stomped to the couch, throwing herself down on it, facing away from him.

He clenched his jaw until it cracked. Her keys cut into his hand.

It was better this way. Better with anger between them.

He left, closing the door and locking it behind him.

Ten minutes later, he was back. With a slightly wilted chicken salad, a piping hot cup of coffee, and the fruit and yogurt cup. It had taken nine of his eleven dollars, but he'd go without lunch himself to make sure Cassidy was fed.

She hadn't moved from the couch. He stood in doorway, wondering if she was still angry and faking it. But a gentle snore drifted out from the living room, making him smile.

Moving softly, he emptied the two bags that contained all the cold things on her list into the refrigerator. Then he placed her salad and yogurt on the top shelf in plain sight. He left the coffee and the rest of the groceries on the counter, along with a note scribbled on the back of her grocery list. *Salad and yogurt in fridge. -T* And he couldn't help it, he scribbled two more words before walking out the door. If her husband saw it, so what. The man should be taking better care of his woman.

CASSIDY SHIFTED NISSA on her hip and slammed her car door shut. A lady in khaki pants and a flowered shirt walked across the small parking lot. It looked like the new lady from the adoption agency. Great. Cassidy had been hoping to at least get in the house and get the kids a snack and settled before she showed up, but court had run longer than she'd expected, then Amy at the day care center had pulled her aside to talk about Jamal...

"Can you grab Nessa's hand, please," Cassidy said to Jamal. Nessa always wanted to walk, while Nissa preferred to be carried. She supposed she should be grateful that only one wanted carried.

Jamal might be having other problems, but she'd always been able to count on him to be an excellent big brother. He spoke in baby talk to Nessa as he led her across the lot.

The lady from the adoption agency intercepted them on the sidewalk in front of the apartment door. Nessa began to cry when Jamal wouldn't let her continue up the apartment steps.

Jamal tried to quiet her by offering her the sippy cup he carried. Over the wailing of the baby, the adoption agency woman held out her hand. "I'm Anne, from Joining Hearts."

"Nice to meet you," Cassidy said and tried to mean it. She wished now she'd cancelled, like she'd been tempted to do when she woke up on the couch at 7:30 this morning still wearing yesterday's clothes and not a thing prepared for her trial. She'd done a ten-minute speed clean on the apartment, given the kids sugary cereal for breakfast, and rushed them out the door, eating the yogurt and fruit that Torque had dropped off last night after she'd fallen asleep. Despite the rush, she'd been smiling and buoyant because of his teasing comment at the bottom of his note. *You snore.* It had made her smile all day long, even though it had been a hectic day and wasn't even close to being done. She still had the sponsor's meeting after she dealt with Anne.

"Come on up. I need to get the kids settled a little, and we can talk."

"That's great. I need to observe you with them anyway, so don't mind me, just do what you normally do."

There was no "normal" in her life, but she didn't bother trying to explain that to Anne. She'd had the twins for two months, and it had been a crazy rocket ride every single day.

They made it to the apartment, with Cassidy ending up carrying both twins and her briefcase, with the diaper bags slung over her shoulders, up both flights of stairs. Better than a gym workout she supposed, but it would have been more relaxing if Anne hadn't been following, occasionally looking around and writing in her notebook.

The stench from her apartment hit her as soon as Jamal unlocked it and pushed the door open. She didn't need to trip over the bag of garbage, although she did, to realize that she'd emptied the can but hadn't remembered to make the extra trip back up to the apartment to carry it down this morning.

That wouldn't have been too horrible, but after she set Nissa down, Jamal tried to help by offering his sister her sippy cup, but he tripped over the garbage bag and knocked into Nissa, and she stumbled and fell, hitting her head on the corner of the counter.

A big blue and red knot immediately formed right in the center of her forehead, and her screams were wild and frantic.

Cassidy's head pounded in sympathetic pain while she held and soothed Nissa. Worrying that maybe she should take Nissa to the ER just to make sure she didn't have brain damage, Cassidy took out the chocolate milk that she'd planned for a Saturday afternoon treat and filled Nissa's sippy cup up with the thick liquid. As soon as she realized it was chocolate milk in her cup, Nissa immediately stopped crying and sucked in blessed quietness.

Chocolate milk wasn't going to make her headache go away, but Cassidy poured Jamal and herself a glass anyway.

She had Nessa's cup filled up and looked around for her. Dismay surged through her chest as she saw that Nessa had taken the unsupervised opportunity to open her briefcase. Her little bottom perched on the garbage bag while court papers and other documents were scattered around her.

Apparently, the garbage bag had leaked, and there was a puddle of smelly goo that the papers that had been in her briefcase were now soaking up. Cassidy gasped and jerked around the counter, knocking over her tall glass of cold chocolate milk. Upon reaching the other side, she saw that the milk was streaming off the bar and flowing directly into her opened purse. She yanked her purse out of the flow, sticking her hand in the now-sloppy interior. She pulled out her cell phone, covered in chocolate milk.

"Don't turn it on," Anne said helpfully from where she sat at the kitchen table, her briefcase neatly by her side, her notebook full of handwriting spread open in front of her. She crossed her legs and reached for her bottle of water. "Dry it out first, then try it."

"Thanks." Cassidy blew a hair out of her face. What had happened to the organized intellectual that was always in control? She didn't even know where to begin. Garbage, papers, phone...at least the twins weren't crying anymore, even if they were sticky and smelly.

As much as she wished for a tub of chocolate chip cookie dough, a super-sized order of cheese fries, and a big chocolate milkshake, it wasn't happening. Not until at least ten o' clock tonight. She had six more hours to survive until then. She rinsed her hands off, rolled up the sleeves of her white blouse, and grabbed a new garbage bag, promising herself a meltdown. Later.

Chapter 6

Torque walked up the hill to Mrs. Angelina Ford's house after spending the morning in Tough's garage. Tough wasn't a big talker—the opposite of Turbo—but he had himself a good setup and a nice little business. He was kind to pay Torque to help, but his shop wasn't busy enough to support two mechanics. That much had been obvious this morning. Not to mention that Tough's customers were gasoline engines and body work. Not diesel.

After Torque kept the promise he made on the bus to visit Mrs. Ford's garage for lunch today, he was going back to the library to apply for more positions. He couldn't take advantage of Tough without at least trying to get a real job.

Torque slowed down as he crested the hill and the house and garage came into sight. Wow. They'd done some major upgrades after he'd gone to prison. The dinky garage was now a large, two-bay building big enough to pull two full-sized tractor trailers into. The paved lot around it would easily hold twenty rigs. The garage sat off to the side at the bottom of a wide, well-maintained lawn.

And the house... Torque vaguely remembered a small ranch, not this huge brick mansion, with a towering center and full windows from top to bottom flanked by two slightly shorter wings on each side. Flaming orange sugar maple trees lined the curved drive to the house.

He stopped and stared. This was the right place, he was sure of it. The lady on the bus, Mrs. Ford, hadn't seemed like a pretentious woman. Hardy stock. A straight-talker. This spread looked like it belonged to a congresswoman from California, not to a diesel mechanic's widow. The man must have done one hen of a business.

Tempted to do a U-turn and take himself right back down the drive, back to the level of people with whom he belonged, Torque walked the rest of the way up, had a small argument with himself about whether he should go to the front door or to the back, followed the path to the back, and knocked on a door that looked like it might lead to the servant's quarters.

Mrs. Ford herself answered. "Watched you walk up the drive, sonny. Where's your car?"

"State's supposed to be sending my license renewal." His old truck, the one from the accident, had been hauled off and probably sold to pay the towing and yard fee. He'd be walking to work until he made enough to buy something he could build.

"Tyke has an old pickup you can use."

"Thanks. I'll think about it." He didn't want to take advantage of an older lady. He also didn't want charity.

Mrs. Ford smiled, like she knew exactly what he was thinking. "Let's go look at the garage. Then we'll come back up and eat lunch. Hungry?"

"Yes, ma'am."

She let him to the side where she had a side-by-side ATV parked. "You drive." She pointed her cane at him before pulling herself into the passenger side and tucking her dress around her legs.

They spent twenty minutes touring the garage that looked like Tyke had just walked out yesterday and it was simply waiting for his return. Fully equipped with all the tools he'd used to do all the diesel repairs, Mrs. Ford explained that no one had touched a thing in the three years that he'd been gone.

"I couldn't stand to do anything with his stuff. He'd been so proud when he finally had enough money to build himself the garage of his dreams. Of course, that was after he'd built the house of mine." Her cheeks pinked, although her eyes grew sad. "I spent a lot of time down here, just sitting with him, keeping him company, quilting." Her voice trailed off like the memories had taken over her thoughts. She shook her head. "Finally, just a few months ago, I decided it was long past time for me to do something here, but I hadn't gotten around to actually doing it. Then I met you."

Torque walked through the big, empty bays and office and parts room, looking but not saying much, and Mrs. Ford didn't press him.

Back at the house, she led him into the dining room, and they sat together, eating soup and salad.

"A couple people have approached me in the past about renting it, but I just wasn't ready. I'd been thinking about selling the house, moving somewhere a little smaller, renting the garage, different things for a while now, then you sat next to me on that bus, and I had a little voice whisper in my ear that you were the one."

Torque hoped she kept the uncomfortable news that she heard voices to herself. It wasn't something that would go over well in society.

"What do you think, son?"

"'Bout what?" Torque said after he swallowed a mouthful of vegetable soup. The kind that wasn't from a can.

"About renting the garage. I can even give you Tyke's customer list. You could reopen his business."

Torque had fallen in love with the garage at first sight, as soon as he crested the little rise in the drive. But it had seemed, and still did, too good to be true.

"What are your terms?"

She named a monthly figure. It seemed high but reasonably so. "And..." She bit her lip and seemed uncertain for the first time. "My daughters said that I should get first and last month's rent upfront, and proof of insurance."

He figured it'd be something like that. The two bucks that he had in his pocket wouldn't even pay for the call to the insurance company, even if he did have money to pay the down payment on a new policy.

He concentrated on the poker face that he'd perfected in prison while he tried to think of a way to come up with the money.

"I could tell you liked the garage."

"I loved it. It's going to make a great business location for someone."

"You."

"I'll have to think about it," Torque hedged, even though he would have to decline her offer, unless the dollar bills in his pocket had been busy having babies all day. Very busy.

The old lady gave him a straight look that reminded him of his gram. "I can't give it to you. My daughters didn't even really like the idea of me offering it to you. They want me to sell."

"I wouldn't let you give it to me."

"I want you to have it."

"I want it."

"Then I'll get the contract drawn up."

"I'll think about it." He couldn't bring himself to say no outright. For some reason, he couldn't tell her, despite the extreme generosity of her offer, he couldn't even afford that much.

"Take a week," she finally said. "Use it for a week. See if you think it's going to work out. If you want it, you can pay me the money next week this time."

The offer was too generous, and Torque should be using the week to look for a job, but it didn't appear Mrs. Ford was going to take no for an answer, so he nodded.

CASSIDY PULLED INTO the back lot of the library, only ten minutes late for the sponsor's meeting. Which, in her opinion, was a small miracle, considering the first five minutes of her adoption meeting were the best five minutes. She'd read some of Anne's notes over her shoulder—"smells like a garbage dump," "children cry incessantly," and "mother seems constantly overwhelmed." All true statements, and they made her feel lower than a night crawler.

She had three minutes from the time Anne left to the time Kelly walked in, and she'd used them to sit on the couch and cuddle all three of her children. There was no way Anne was going to recommend that the adoption agency allow Cassidy to keep the twins let alone give Cassidy a green light to adopt the twins. She felt like she'd let the kids down. Nissa and Nessa and, most of all, Jamal, just because she hadn't been able to pull it all together and make a good impression.

Anne hadn't even asked about her so-called serious boyfriend.

Thankfully, she'd been able to text Kelly in time, and Kelly had brought cans of SpaghettiOs for the kids for supper.

Taking a deep breath, she set what was left of the chicken salad that Torque had bought yesterday aside. She'd been eating it with her fingers as she drove across town, and all that was left was a few pieces of lettuce. She grabbed a folder from the front seat. It basically had nothing but blank paper in it, since all her papers had been in her briefcase and were ruined. Her briefcase smelled like a dumpster in July, and it was the only one she had.

A little spike of anticipation shot through her. Torque would be here. She tried to push it aside, but it just grew. Maybe he hated her, but there was no way she could return the feeling. Even before he took her punishment, she'd never been able to find anyone who compared to him. Not at her prestigious private school. Not at college. Not at law school.

Shoving the folder under her arm, she rolled her sleeves back down and buttoned the cuffs, hurrying to the back door of the library conference room.

Seven people and the coordinator were already seated around the large, glossy wood conference table. She recognized two ex-cons as people she'd defended, and several of the business people were familiar as well, but her eyes were drawn, like a compass needle to true north, to

WHAT HE WANTS

Torque. He sprawled in his seat. Even next to the other parolees, his broad shoulders stood out. His ball cap sat on the table in front of him. His eyes tracked her progress around the room to the seat beside him.

"Miss Kimball. You just missed the introductions." Frank Bigelough was the coordinator for the pilot project. There was plenty of irritation and a slight hint of accusation in his tone.

She schooled her features, hiding the ping of another failure in her chest.

"I'm sorry," Cassidy said in her most professional tone as she pulled out her chair. "I had a meeting that ran over." She gave her professional smile and sat, glancing at Torque as she did so.

"You eat?" he asked in a low tone that flowed under Frank's monologue coming from the head of the table.

She nodded. "The chicken salad you brought. Thanks."

He jerked his head. They both turned back to Frank, who stood at the head of the table and outlined the guidelines for the voluntary program.

"This is a professional relationship between you and your mentor. Their job is to guide you, give you real life advice and support, be a reference for you as you apply for jobs, and in some cases, they or their employers have agreed to hire you and they'll be your coworkers and supervisors. Basically, they're here to ease your integration back into society."

Frank paced with his hands behind his back. "Those are the mentors' responsibilities. The parolees' responsibilities are just as important. These mentors have agreed to put their reputations on the line for you. They've agreed to give of their time and expertise to help you. Your job is to respect that and make sure that you do your best to live up to the expectations placed on you. The success of our program, and its entire future, depends on you. If word gets out that you are taking advantage of your mentors, or anything of that nature, then you will be sabotaging any other parolee's opportunity to participate in this program."

He stopped and faced the table. "Is that clear to everyone?"

People nodded and murmured "yes."

"Good." He resumed pacing. "You will have a rap sheet for the rest of your life. But this program is designed to take some of the sting out of that. We're hoping that it will develop the reputation of producing well-adjusted, law-abiding citizens. Potential employers will see this on your resume, and it will negate your ex-con status. Participants have been carefully chosen for your ability to do well in the program and because of a judge's, an attorney's, or a mentor's recommendation. I have high expectations for everyone."

"Now, we'll start here on my right hand and go around the table. Each pair can tell the group about your first session together and your plans for this next year of mentorship, and I think it would also be beneficial if each mentor talked about the positive qualities in your matched parolee that led you to volunteer to be their mentor."

Cassidy swallowed as the first pair began speaking. She should have been more prepared. Not only did she now feel like a failure as a mother and, after today's disastrous performance in court, as a public defender, but she was letting Torque down too. Maybe her parents and her classmates in high school had been right. She was just a pretty face. Good for homecoming queen, good for modeling. And, yeah, she got her law degree and passed the bar, but when it came right down to it, she couldn't actually handle a real life. She could only look good in front of the camera.

TORQUE WASN'T ACQUAINTED with anyone in the room. A couple of people he knew by name, but his attention was on Cassidy. One side of her shirt was untucked, and her hair was lopsided. The circles under her eyes, which yesterday had been a faint print, were well-defined today. Exhaustion tightened her eyes and mouth. Always slender, her clothes seemed extra loose.

Yesterday, she'd mentioned a court hearing and underwear briefs. He'd guess that neither went well today.

He hadn't wanted to show up to the meeting, but after hearing what Frank had said, he appreciated Cassidy's work with getting him into this. It would be a backup for him if things with Angelina Ford and her husband's shop didn't work out. No job that he'd applied for had called him back, and he figured it must be the ex-con status on his application that made them shy away. If this program was designed to help with that, it could only be a good thing. It had already helped him. He hadn't considered putting Cassidy down for a reference.

None of the pairs were taking a long time to talk, so maybe this meeting wouldn't be as long and as boring as he'd feared. Actually, he wasn't bored. There was no way he could sit beside Cassidy and be bored. All she had to do was enter the room and every cell in his body was on alert. It had always been like that. Now, with her beside him, close enough that he could uncross his ankles and bump her leg with his, or lean forward and brush her arm, it was impossible to focus on anything else.

He could hold her hand under the table. Except...he couldn't. His heart dropped, and his lungs deflated. How could she have gotten married to someone else? And so soon? He'd tossed and turned over those questions all night.

But what had he expected? They weren't a couple. Hadn't ever been a couple. They'd spent some time together, taken a few rides, but he'd never asked her to be his steady girlfriend. Like she would have even considered it. He had nothing to offer her, and they were too young anyway.

He had no rights to her or with her.

Finally, as he had thought about it, he had to admit what really bothered him. He'd made a major sacrifice for her, and he'd expected her to be grateful. If not to wait for him, to at least give some nod to the fact that he served her time. Maybe to have made an extra effort to make something out of her life, to do good, to...he didn't know.

But it was wrong on his part. He'd volunteered, and he'd given her no choice. He hadn't asked for anything or done it because he expected payment. So, he needed to let it go. And he probably could. Except the husband thing really bothered him. How could he stand to be around Cassidy when he ached for her to be his, and yet he couldn't touch her, protect her, help her? But had to stand by while another man neglected her and took advantage of her.

He didn't want to be stuck with Cassidy at arm's length, not for the next year, not for the next meeting. He couldn't stand it. The attraction he felt for her was too strong, but to do anything but ignore it went against every moral belief he had. He couldn't be that man. Not if he wanted to look himself in the mirror every morning.

The pair beside him finished talking, and it was their turn. He waited for Cassidy to start. She clasped her hands together on the table and looked around. Then she looked at her hands. Her voice, when she finally spoke, was somehow frail. "I chose Torque because I knew him before he went to prison. He is hardworking and honest, honorable and loyal. I felt the judge was unfairly harsh in his sentencing, and I wanted to do something to help him. He deserves it."

Torque's gut squeezed. His heart thumped slow and hard.

She looked around the room, everywhere but at him.

"I fought to be able to mentor a man, even though other leaders suggested it wasn't a good idea to have male and female pairs. But I knew that Torque is moral and upright."

She blew out a deep, shaky breath. Flashbacks of their nights together rolled through his head. He didn't know if she knew how badly he'd wanted to do more than what they'd done.

"I bungled our first meeting when he was released. I bungled our second even worse." Her knuckles whitened on the table in front of her.

"I...I'm actually not sure I can be the mentor that Torque deserves. I think it might be wise to find someone else to take my place."

"I'm not doing this without you." The words came out low, without a thought from him. It was exactly the opposite of what he'd wanted five minutes ago, but after her short speech, it was the only thing he could say.

She finally looked at him, shaking her head, her blue eyes troubled and dejected. Her shoulders slumped. "I can't."

He straightened out of his slouch, planting his boots on the floor and leaning forward, toward her. "You're the smartest person in this room, so much more than a pretty face attached to a body that looks great on camera." He couldn't stand to see her discouraged. It rubbed his heart raw. "Our first meeting wasn't a disaster. I had a bad attitude, and I'm apologizing for it now. Our second meeting was actually quite informative for me."

Her brows furrowed, and she looked at him suspiciously.

He held his hands up. "Not everyone can steer a shopping cart with a hip and a knee. I tried to do that after you left the store yesterday, and it's harder than it looks."

Titters drifted out around the table.

Cassidy's lips twitched.

"If you quit, I quit too." He folded his hands together to keep from reaching for her and stared her down.

She looked away first.

Frank cleared his throat. "That was, um, interesting." He raised his brows and looked out over his glasses. "So are you two in or out?"

Cassidy swallowed, the white column of her neck moving. Torque looked away because he could suddenly almost feel his lips right there, along the graceful curve of her throat.

What in the world had he just done? He'd decided he couldn't work with Cassidy, and like she'd read his mind, she'd quit, giving him the opportunity to have the benefits of the program without the impossible temptation of her presence, and he'd just destroyed the whole thing.

He lifted his brows.

She raised her chin. Her lips tilted.

"We're in," she said.

Chapter 7

The meeting ended soon after, and Torque waited while she picked up her folder and said a few words to Frank. He walked out beside her casually. She'd always loved walking beside him. He was one of the few people she knew that she had to look up to. He made her feel feminine, in a powerful way. He didn't crowd her or grab her, but somehow, they felt evenly matched. Not even, but equal. Like they fit together.

She waited until they were near her car and away from the other pairs. "I'm sorry I quit on you so publicly."

"I'm kinda used to it."

She stopped, jerking her head around. "What?"

He held his hands up. "Kidding. You seem down."

"I had a day from hell."

"Hmm. Never had one of those."

She eyed him. His face, as usual, gave nothing away.

"Okay. Maybe when the judge said I had ten years in the pen." He lifted his lips, and she could hardly believe he was joking about it.

Placing her hands on her hips, she said, "That wasn't fair. I could never figure out why he did that."

"Gram seemed to think he had some kind of thing against our family. His sentence was harsh, but still within the guidelines."

"How does it feel? Being out?" She wanted to connect with him, somehow. At least he was talking to her some.

His expression closed down, and he looked over her shoulder. She didn't think he was going to answer. Then, he crossed his arms over his chest and said, "It's a little scary, actually. After having someone take complete care of you for ten years, now, all the sudden, it's up to me if I eat or not. It's harder than I thought."

"You'd rather be back in?" she asked incredulously.

He snorted. "'Course not."

Even though she couldn't help him in his field of diesel repair, she tried to focus on what she could help with. "You have been putting me down for a reference?"

"No. Never thought of it."

"Make sure you do that from now on." Stubborn man. "Have you gotten a job yet?"

He shifted, leaning against her car, his eyes following the other attendees as they walked to their rides. "I visited Mrs. Ford today. She offered to let me set up shop in her husband's old garage. Actually, it's pretty new. He just had that and the big new house built before he died."

Cassidy could hardly keep from jumping up and down. It was a great offer, and one that suited Torque perfectly. "You should take her up on it."

"Can't. Don't have the money to put down on rent."

If that was all it was. "Let me loan it to you." She hadn't touched her trust fund. Probably she was still getting money from the family pickle business, but she had handed over all the info to her accountant and hadn't touched a thing since Torque went up. Now that he was out...

He gave her a long, hard look. "No."

Of course. "I knew you were going to say that. What I don't understand is why."

"I don't know." He looked away.

"I'm calling her tomorrow. I'm sending her a check. You were born to do diesel repair in your own shop."

"If I did that, I wouldn't have a regular paycheck. I'd have to advertise." He shoved his hands in his pockets and brought out two one-dollar bills and some change. "This is all I have in the world."

She stared at the money, trying to hide her shock. It could have been her, if she didn't have the family she did and if he hadn't taken her place. "You realize that if you hadn't done what you did, our positions would be reversed right now?"

"No, they wouldn't."

That was probably true. The judge wouldn't have given her as harsh of a sentence. But it was a gamble Torque had taken. And lost.

"It doesn't matter," he finally said.

"No, you're right. My sentence wouldn't have been as long. My parents have money, and when I got out, they would have showered me with it. I wouldn't have the struggle you have right now." She put her hand on his arm. "That's why I want to help."

He breathed out heavily and stared into the darkness, as though pulling the words he needed from deep inside him. "If I take your money... If I let you help..." He hooked a hand around his neck and twisted away, before coming back, leaning down, coming closer. Holding his hands up, he said, fierce but soft, "I need to build whatever I have with these." He shook his hands. "It needs to be mine. It can't be ours. There is no 'us.' I have to do it." He slapped his chest.

His agony tore at her soul. She forced her words out. "Plenty of men build businesses with money they borrow from the bank."

"That's different."

"How?"

"They pay the bank back. The bank doesn't give them money just because they did a good deed. It's not a good deed anymore if someone pays you for it."

She saw his point, but it still hurt that he was pushing her away so harshly. "I'll give you a loan. We'll have a contract drawn up, and you'll pay me back with interest."

He stood staring down at her, his eyes dark and unreadable under the brim of his cap.

"It's pride that's keeping you from accepting."

"Yeah. Didn't have much of anything else for the last ten years. Pride. Faith." He opened his mouth like he was going to add something else but then closed it.

"Pride, faith, and what?" she prompted.

He shook his head then answered, "Pride, faith, and a dream that ended up being a mirage."

AFTER TOSSING AND TURNING in his old bed in his gram's small trailer, Torque got up before the sun and walked up the hill to the big brick mansion.

Yesterday, Cassidy was only half-right. Pride was part of it. But he'd figured out as he tossed and turned that fear was the other part. He'd spent all those years in prison being beaten down, told he was the dregs of society, no-good, a blight on his family's name, and all kinds of other things. Even though he hadn't even done what he was in there for, it was hard, almost impossible to come out with even a ghost of his former confidence.

When he'd been seventeen, he'd dreamed that he'd start his own business, be successful. So successful that someday he'd walk up bold as brass to Cassidy's father's house, knock on the door, and ask permission to court his daughter. Court her. He wasn't interested in dating. He was interested in marriage. That was his dream.

It would never happen now.

But he could still work toward the other part of that. Owning a successful business. Cassidy was right. Plenty of people started off in debt. He'd never borrowed money before. Gram had always said "the borrower is servant to the lender."

But he couldn't pass up such a great opportunity. Not when everything had lined up and all he had to do was take the risk. Ditch the pride, fight the fear, and the dream could be his.

He was going to tell Mrs. Ford now, work at going over the books and accounts and checking the inventory in the garage today, and spend the week working his butt off. Opportunities didn't come to people who sat around, afraid.

CASSIDY SLID INTO HER car as dusk fell. Court ran late again, and she had to meet with one of her clients afterwards. She was already exhausted, and even though she looked forward to picking up her children and spending some quality time with them, finally, she wasn't sure how she was going to have the energy to make it to bedtime, with all the things that they would need: homework with Jamal and any behavioral issues. Baths for the twins. Supper, that she hoped to cook herself, but it was tempting to stop at the store and buy a frozen pizza.

At least on the way to the day care, she could return the Joining Hearts call. Anne's boss, Larissa, had left a message along with her personal cell number.

She answered on the fourth ring. Cassidy put her phone on speaker.

"Thanks for returning my call, Cassidy." Larissa sighed. "Anne's report was not very encouraging."

Cassidy let out a laugh that had more nerves than she wanted to show in it. "She caught me on a really bad day."

"She said you said it was a typical day."

"Well, yes. I mean, of course, life with toddlers is always interesting."

"It is," Larissa said compassionately. "And life with twins is exceptionally hard." Papers rustled before her voice came back on. "Anne said that your eight-year-old, Jamal, spent a lot of time helping you. We don't like to see that—parents relying on the older children to do the work of a parent."

Cassidy tried to gather her defenses. She was trained to argue, after all. But she hadn't expected the complaint to come from that angle.

"Jamal enjoys helping with his sisters."

"Of course he does. But he needs to be a typical eight-year-old. Not your personal nanny. I don't want to sound unkind. I know children are a hard job." She sighed. "Pennsylvania law does not require there to be two parents in an adoptive house. And we allowed you to adopt Jamal as a single mom. However, it's our agency's policy, and I believe my recommendation is going to be that the twins go to a two-parent home. It's too much work for one person. Then to add Jamal into the mix. You just can't do it by yourself."

"I could hire a nanny. I've actually seriously considered it." She could afford it. She had made a pledge while Torque was behind bars that she would not live a lavish lifestyle as long as he lived in a prison, doing her time. It wasn't right. She'd kept her pledge, driving an old car, renting a cheap apartment in a bad section of town, buying her clothes at the local discount store. No housekeeper, no nanny, no meal service or maid.

"The children don't need a nanny. They need a mother who has time for them. And with twins, they need a mother and a father." Larissa's voice was firm.

Cassidy's fingers squeezed the steering wheel. "What about Jamal? He loves his sisters. Doesn't he deserve to grow up with his flesh-and-blood siblings?"

There was a pause. Cassidy had met Larissa several times, and she really did have a heart. She also had the best interests of the children first and foremost. She cared about Jamal and his desire to be with his sisters. Cassidy held her breath.

"You're right. I want Jamal to know his sisters. And we constantly search for families who are willing to take multiple siblings. We also always give precedence to adoptive families who have already adopted siblings, as you have with Jamal. But, Cassidy, it's too much for a single mom. A nanny is a good idea, but it's not a stable answer." She paused. "I have a note here that you were in a serious relationship. Anne said she didn't ask and you never mentioned it, but that there was no man there with you. Is that true? Is there a possibility that there could be a father in the picture?"

Immediately Cassidy thought of Torque. If her life were her own, she might pursue him, hoping that someday he might feel something for her. Even half of what she felt for him would be more than most people lived on. But there were two impassible roadblocks. She was his mentor, and there couldn't even be a hint of a romantic relationship between them, and...Torque's ex-con status, while not specifically against Pennsylvania law, would almost certainly be a roadblock. Maybe if he'd been out for a couple of years...

"Miss Kimball?"

"I'm sorry." She pulled slowly into the day care parking lot. "I really am sorry. I actually do have a man. A boyfriend. Serious boyfriend." She cleared her throat. She'd never been a good liar. "Yeah. Um. In order to foster the children, do we have to be married, or could we be living together?"

"It needs to be a stable relationship. If you've just recently moved in together, we'd want to do an interview with the two of you. We'd want to know information that could help us assess the longevity and seriousness of the relationship. Of course, if you adopted, he would have joint custody, just as with any children, so you wouldn't want to make a spur-of-the-moment decision." A delicate pause. "You do have someone?"

"Yes. I do. We haven't spoken much about children, though."

"Would you like to schedule an appointment for the two of you together to come to the office, or should you discuss this with him, first?"

"Officially, I'm fostering the twins right now. How much time do I have before you give them to another foster family or start to look at other couples as prospective parents?"

"Oh, honey." Her voice had a smile in it. "We're already looking. The sooner we can get those sweet babies settled in their forever home, the better. That's what we all want—children settled in a safe environment with loving parents nurturing and protecting them."

"Of course. That's what I want, too." It really was. But she could provide everything they needed and keep the siblings together.

"As for fostering...I know you want the best for the children, that Jamal is their brother, and that you love them. I know that, but I also know that what you're trying to do is too much for one person." Silence on the line for a few heartbeats. "Okay, here's what we'll do. Call me back when you know about your boyfriend. After our team meets together, I will let you know our final decision. I felt it only fair to warn you today about what that decision is probably going to be."

"I appreciate it."

Cassidy put her head down on the steering wheel. She'd just lied, which she hated. There was no boyfriend. No possibility of a boyfriend. She'd had plenty of men chase her over the years. Because of her pretty face and model's body, she supposed, since it was hard to get any of them to engage in a conversation or to care about anything other than the latest sports statistics. Maybe she'd been burned too many times, but she never felt sure that any man wanted her for anything more than her looks. People said she was beautiful. She just saw herself when she looked in the mirror.

Torque was the only man who ever seemed to think there was a brain and emotions that went along with her looks. Even though, he, more than any other man, made her feel beautiful. Inside and out.

But she wasn't going down that road. Couldn't go down that road.

There wasn't anyone else. She could pay someone to act, but it would turn into a nightmare, legally. Not to mention she could go to jail, be disbarred, and lose the girls anyway.

She knocked her forehead against the steering wheel. There had to be a way to keep the girls. There just had to be.

She wouldn't allow herself to wallow, and she wouldn't take this lying down. She'd fight for her children.

Chapter 8

Torque slammed the hood shut and handed Rex the filter wrench. "Thanks, dude," Rex said.

"Hey, no problem," Torque answered and meant it.

He'd been leaning against Cassidy's apartment building while Rex was struggling to change the oil in his Oldsmobile. After walking over and offering to help, Torque had basically done it himself, since Rex was trying to watch a YouTube video while following the steps. Time had flown by while his hands were occupied. But now... Where was she? It had gotten dark a while ago. Rex and he had finished up by the pole light in the front corner of the lot.

He should probably go home, but he wanted to meet with his mentor and tell her that he was opening a garage, for the next week at least. Who was he trying to fool? He wanted to see Cassidy, and that was the only excuse he could come up with.

A chilly breeze blew, rustling the leaves. It was getting colder, too. He needed to buy some winter clothes soon. His pants still fit around the waist, although they were an inch or two too short, but his sweatshirts and jackets were way too narrow to squeeze his shoulders into.

"You wanna come up to my apartment? I'll get ya a cold one," Rex said as he smacked his hands together.

"Nah. Thanks anyway." It occurred to Torque that this could be Cassidy's husband. He studied the guy. Slightly balding on top, easy smile, baggy jeans. It was hard to picture Cassidy with him. He saw her more with a business type. Maybe someone whose airplane was just now landing at the airport. Maybe Cassidy and the kids were picking him up, since it was Friday. Maybe she was married to a doctor. A surgeon. That would explain why he was never around, although it made the rundown apartment she had not make any sense. Hardly a doctor's digs.

"'Preciate the help." Rex slapped Torque's shoulder and walked away, disappearing through the front door of the apartment complex.

Torque had settled himself back in his earlier position, one shoulder leaning against the building wall, legs crossed, hands in his pockets, when headlights cut through the lot and he recognized the hum of Cassidy's motor the way another person might have recognized her voice.

He stayed in his place. If her husband was with her, he wasn't going to rush in. It wasn't his place.

But she got out alone, immediately opening the back door and reaching in for a twin. Torque pushed off the wall and ambled over to the other side. He'd never touched a car seat before, but he was pretty good at figuring out how to work things.

Cassidy's head snapped up when he opened the door.

"Torque?"

His lips twitched. She said it like she wasn't quite sure it was him. Did he look like someone else she knew?

"Wanted to talk."

Her fingers stilled. "Is everything okay?"

"Yeah."

"Do you mind if I get the kids in and start feeding them?"

"Figured I'd help."

To his surprise, her eyes filled before her jaw clenched and she looked back at the little girl who was pulling on her hair. What would have caused *that* reaction? Bad day?

He didn't say anything but put his fingers on the car seat latch and worked on figuring it out. The little girl with the tight black curls and sparkling black eyes scrunched up her nose, not sure if she liked the big stranger leaning over her. Torque figured she wanted out of her car seat more than she wanted to protest the invasion of her space because her face straightened out and she grabbed his nose.

"She likes to get peoples' noses," Jamal said from the back seat.

One finger was actually up his nose, and her nails were kind of sharp, but he'd rather deal with a thousand sharp fingernails than one crying child, so he gritted his teeth and answered Jamal. "If that was a warning, it was a little late."

Jamal's teeth flashed white. The latch popped, and Torque carefully lifted the armrest over the baby's head.

"Good thing you're doing Nessa. Nissa doesn't like anyone but Mom to hold her."

Torque plucked the baby from the seat and stood. She stiffened her body immediately, and the cuddly, soft baby of a minute ago became a stiff board.

"She likes to walk," Jamal said with the wisdom of an older brother.

"I see." He set her down, her chubby legs churning as soon as her little feet hit the blacktop. He snagged her hand.

"I'll get the baby bag. She wants to be first to the door." Jamal stuck his head in the car.

"Hmm." Torque wasn't sure how Jamal knew all that, but Torque wasn't going to argue. His experience with babies was limited to...whatever he remembered from his own and his brothers' childhoods.

He was right, though. She raced through the parking lot so fast Torque half-expected to see black smoke leaking out her diaper. Stopping at the steps, she let out a howl, apparently because the door didn't magically open in front of her.

"Here," Cassidy called. He turned and reflexively snatched the keys that she'd thrown out of midair. "You can take them up." She stuck her head back in the car, pulling a newish-looking briefcase out.

Jamal stood behind him, a baby bag slung over one narrow shoulder and a book bag slung over the other.

"Let's go. This is heavy," Jamal said.

Torque opened the door and got pulled through by the little bulldozer holding his hand. He had to smile at her tenacity. The steps were a little big for her, but he found if he lifted up, just a little, on her arm, she could do the rest herself.

Jamal went over to her other side and held that hand. Torque could see how that would make everything go faster, but Jamal had trouble keeping the baby bag and book bag from slipping off his shoulders.

"Give me that." Torque reached over and took the baby bag, which was surprisingly heavy, like it contained a rebuild kit for a B-model Mack.

"Mom says she's gonna be doing these steps all by herself soon, but someone will still have to be behind her so she doesn't fall and hurt herself."

"Good idea." Because the question was burning a hole in his tongue, he spit it out. "Where's your dad?"

Jamal shrugged. "Prison, I think."

Torque blinked. Holy frig.

Jamal chattered while they finished climbing the stairs. Cassidy had caught up with them by the time he'd reached the door and unlocked it, remembering the key from the other night. The little steam engine beside him was still tugging on his hand, but he hardly noticed.

The father of Cassidy's children was in prison. And he'd never in his life unlocked a door with children at his feet and a woman at his back, like they were all a family waiting to go into their home and spend the evening together. Intense longing like he'd never felt before slammed through his body with the unstoppable force of a forty-ton truck.

"Are you okay? You swayed, like you are having a dizzy spell." Cassidy's voice from behind him grounded him back in reality. Except no one ever asked him if he were okay.

"Fine." He pushed the door open.

The next couple of hours went by in what felt like a few minutes' dream. He lay on the living room floor, playing with all three kids while Cassidy made the whole house smell delicious.

They ate together, sitting on opposite sides of her small table, each of them feeding a twin. Occasionally their gaze met over the table, and he wondered as he searched her eyes if she felt as if she were having an out-of-body experience too. If it felt surreal to her to be sitting across from each other, the chatter of kids and the occasional whine just background noise. His every focus was on Cassidy.

She smiled and chatted with the kids like she'd done it all her life.

She gave Jamal adult answers to his questions. They talked about his day at school.

She directed a couple of Jamal's questions to him, and he found himself offering to take the boy to the garage and teach him how to do some simple car maintenance. He said they'd go to Tough's and get tires on his mom's car.

Cassidy smiled even bigger the more he talked to Jamal.

Torque's heart swelled, feeling like it would burst. The hair on his arms stood up, and it got harder and harder to look away each time their eyes met.

She wasn't wearing a ring.

He and Jamal cleared off the table. Torque did the dishes while Jamal did his homework and Cassidy gave the twins a bath.

She brought them out to the kitchen, each dressed in outfits that covered them from toes to neck. They were shiny and smelled better than anything he'd ever smelled except for Cassidy. One of the little ones, the one on Cassidy's right hip, held her arms out to him.

"Nessa wants you," Jamal stated. Torque dried the dishwater off his hands and reached out for the little one. She grinned up at him, showing all two teeth in her mouth, and then her chubby baby arms went around his neck. Like she'd reached into his chest and grabbed it, his heart slid into her hand. He lay his cheek on her head, nuzzling the puffy softness of her hair. His eyes started to close. Just before they shut completely, he saw Cassidy's face. Her unguarded expression, full of love and longing, pierced his soul.

"Come on back," she said softly. "You can lay her down." She looked down at Jamal. "Finished?"

"Yep. Torque checked it. He said it was okay."

"Take a quick shower and brush your teeth. I'll be in to kiss you good night in a minute." She turned and led the way back the short hall to a dimly lit room. Two cribs hugged one wall. A small bed, that Torque realized after a minute must be hers, rested against the opposite wall. Two dressers filled the room to bursting. There was barely enough room for him to squeeze between the cribs and the bed.

"That one." She pointed to the farthest crib in. He watched her set the other twin down and imitated her movements. Both babies whimpered a little as they settled in.

Torque's arms felt cold and empty. Funny how ninety seconds of holding a baby could make such an impression.

Cassidy stood between the door and him. Without giving it any thought, Torque took the short step that separated them. He leaned down. "You're not married to their dad?" He meant to ask gently, but the words came out harsh and low.

"No," she said. Her face turned up to him, but he couldn't read her eyes or see her expression.

He didn't think about it. He took a small step forward and slid his arm around her shoulders. She melted into him immediately. His other hand came up, and he dropped his face into her hair, inhaling deeply. Her body, tall and slim, fit perfectly against his. It always had. But he kept his arms on her shoulders and didn't try to pull her closer. Just holding her was enough for now. More than he ever thought he'd have again.

A delicate little snore interrupted their peaceful interlude.

She pulled away, and he didn't try to keep her.

His hands fell. Their arms slid down. Her hand caught his and held. She tugged, a little more gently than her daughter had. He followed just as easily.

"Come on," she whispered, pulling him out of the room and carefully shutting the door behind them. "I always read Jamal a story."

"I have all night." His voice floated out of his throat, low and deep and wishing.

He stood in the doorway while she chatted for a few minutes with Jamal. Then she picked up a book, turned to the page marked with a bookmark, and read a chapter.

He'd heard about families like this. Families that read together. Ate together. Did things together. He never thought to be part of one.

He wasn't part of one, he reminded himself roughly. Just watching. He hadn't expected to stay this long.

They prayed together, and she kissed Jamal on the forehead before standing up and flicking off the light.

He backed into the hall, and she slipped out, closing the door. She stood close again. He breathed deeply of her scent, pulling it in, craving more. He fisted his hands to keep from reaching for her, drawing her to him. Wanting her like the last ten years had never happened. Like they were teens again and she was all he thought about day and night. She was in every motor he worked on. The glint of sunlight on metal like her flashing eyes, the softness of polished aluminum like her skin, cylindric pistons like her slender legs. Big diesel motors and Cassidy, he'd spent years with his brain full of both.

He realized they just stood in the dark hall. Close but not touching. Hearing each breath. His mind full of memories, his hands aching to hold her again. His heart thumping painfully, weeping for every second he'd lost with her.

But his twenty-eight-year-old mind was a little smarter and slightly less susceptible to his raging hormones than his seventeen-year-old mind had been.

She'd moved on with someone else and hadn't wasted any time. He couldn't stand the pain of watching her walk away from him again.

He'd had an enjoyable evening, but he was here on business. It was time he got down to it.

"You have a minute to talk to me?" His words came out with a sharp edge.

"Yes." She led him back to the kitchen.

Chapter 9

"Tea or coffee?" Cassidy asked, proud that her voice did not tremble. Having Torque in her home, beside her, helping with her kids, his presence at once overwhelming and soothing, had been so much more than she'd hoped or dreamed.

She shouldn't have done it. She risked his future with the mentor program, and she owed him a fresh start. A better start.

Plus, she had to figure out something with her kids. That was more important than anything else. No matter how amazing it had felt to be almost like a family with Torque.

She eyed him as he leaned a hip against the counter, two mugs set down in front of him. He'd be a great dad. Patient. Considerate. Hands on.

Her eyes dropped to his hands. He'd had them in dishwater earlier. Big, strong hands, with long, capable fingers. Tough enough to earn a living, but they could be careful too. She remembered the gentleness of his hands. She shivered and gripped the coffeepot carefully. He didn't move as she stepped closer and poured the brown liquid into both cups.

She set the pot down and placed cream and sugar on the counter. He didn't touch them. She poured cream into her cup, the clink of her spoon as she stirred the only sound. Somehow the air around her felt heavy.

"I'm sitting, if you don't mind." She carried her cup to the table. He followed silently, sitting across from her. Their knees bumped under the table. His expression didn't change. She moved her leg.

"You wanted to talk," she prompted.

He looked down at his coffee, then his dark brown eyes drilled into hers. "Where's your man?"

"This is what you came to talk about?" Heat climbed up her neck. She wanted to feel outrage that he would be so nosy, but she buried her nose in her coffee cup. Why would his question embarrass her?

Maybe because it was so direct. His brother Tough barely talked at all. Torque wasn't that quiet, but he never wasted words.

"No." He put his hands on the table, next to his cup but not touching it. She'd noticed his tendency, a new one since she'd known him before, of spreading his hands out in plain sight. "But the question occurred to me, since every time I see you, you're doing the work of three people by yourself."

She sighed. "After I graduated from law school and landed the county defender's position here in Brickly Springs, I fostered Jamal for a year before adopting him this past spring. His mother had the twins, and once Jamal found out about them, he begged to be with his sisters." She twisted her coffee cup around. "They've allowed me to foster them."

The tension seemed to drain out of him, and he looked more relaxed than she'd seen him since he'd gotten out. Still, he prompted her. "But?"

"But yesterday they made a home visit, and I found out today they feel it's best if the twins go to a home with a mother *and* a father."

"You're not gonna take that sitting down."

Her head snapped up. Even after all the years apart, he knew her so well.

He wasn't looking at her though, seeming to find his coffee cup extremely interesting. Finally, he picked it up and took several big swallows. When he set it down, it was almost empty.

She stared at her own mug, lost in thought. What could she do to convince them to let her keep the twins? There had to be a way.

"You're a lawyer."

"Yes. You sound surprised."

"On the ride home from Pittsburgh, I saw you..." He paused there, his eyes never leaving hers.

The heat that had crept up her neck earlier hit the flash point and burst into flames. Her entire body burned. She knew exactly what he was talking about, she could read it all in his eyes. Admiration. Confusion. Even jealousy. Lust burned there too. Banked. But hotter and deeper than the other emotions.

"...Hard to miss." He blinked slowly. His mouth flattened. "I assumed you were a model."

"Modeling earned me money in college and law school."

"You're more than a pretty face."

"I've had to fight to prove that to everyone but you."

"Parents cut you off?"

"I cut myself off, I guess you could say."

His head tilted a miniscule amount. She read the question in that tilt and found she wanted to give him the answer. "After I found out your sentence, I couldn't eat or sleep. My grades dropped, and I almost quit school. The guilt was overwhelming. That you were where you were, and I was living, maybe not the high life, but a life of ease, for sure."

His eye twitched. "That was the point."

"I hated it. I hated myself." She laughed without humor. "I had a lot of hate. Guilt. Self-loathing."

He made a noise, and she looked at him, but he didn't say anything, didn't move.

She continued. "I did a few other things," the least of which was to visit Miss Betty, whose husband she had killed in the crash, "but basically, I stopped living like a spoiled rich girl, spent only what was necessary, got a job—modeling—and..."

He stood abruptly, his chair flying backwards and landing with a crash on its back. "That's why you're living in this dump."

She eyed him as he paced to the counter, slamming his hand down on it.

"Basically, you've been living below the poverty line since I went up."

She stood slowly. He wasn't going to intimidate her with his anger, whatever the cause. "I bought a new outfit before I went to pick you up. They were the first new clothes I'd bought for myself since the day you were sentenced."

His teeth ground together. A vein in his temple throbbed.

"I assume you hadn't bought anything either." She tilted her head and tried to smile.

He breathed through his nose. In and out. Slow drags.

She couldn't stand it. She stomped a foot on the floor and crossed her arms over her chest. "Why are you angry? Doesn't it bother you to think that you were inside, your life on hold, and it should have been me? Wouldn't you be happier to think that I wasn't running around living the high life?"

"No."

She threw her hands up. "Then why did you do it? I never understood. Couldn't ever figure out why you sent me away and lied about the whole thing." Her voice was raised to a pitch she never used when the twins were sleeping, but she barely noticed. "You knew exactly what was going to happen. Maybe you didn't think the sentence would be so long or that you'd serve it all, but you knew. Still, you stayed that night and took my place. Why, Torque?"

He shook his head. Either he couldn't or wouldn't tell her.

Maybe her anger had drained away some of his. He lifted a finger and brushed a hair away from her face, allowing his finger to slide down her cheek. He cupped her jaw. She closed her eyes, fighting for breath.

"It wasn't so that both of us had to suffer," he said, his voice even and low.

"I couldn't be free as a bird, with no cares in the world, while you sat in a cell for me. I had to make those years count for both of us." Her words came out through clenched teeth, her eyes still closed.

"You got your law degree. That's not slouching."

"I felt guilty," she whispered.

A heavy pause filled the room. He breathed out. "Me too."

Her eyes popped open.

"I could have stopped the truck, Cassidy. Look at us." He found her hand, pressing the palm against his, lifting them up and comparing them. "Your will might be as strong as mine, but I wasn't sitting helpless in the passenger seat."

"So why didn't you?"

He dropped her hand and looked over her head. "Loved seeing you drive my truck." He swallowed. "Did something to my chest to see you sitting behind the wheel. You looked so happy." His hand came back up, gently cupping her cheek. "I never wanted to hurt anyone. Least of all you. But I wasn't able to resist you. Never have been."

Her heart flipped, and her stomach clenched. Heat pooled in her belly, low and deep.

"Nor I, you." She leaned into his hand. "Why were you angry? What do you want from me?"

He shook his head. "It doesn't matter. I always wanted more than you could give. Still do."

"Whatever it is, I'll give it. Whatever it takes."

He put a finger over her lips. "Shh." He watched as his finger traced the outline of her lips. "You're right. There isn't any money in the world that could pay for what I did. I don't want money, never have."

"Then, what?" she asked. Her tongue slipped out to touch his finger.

He hissed.

"Can't ask for it. Can't demand it. It has to be freely given, or it's not worth anything."

"What?" she cried, frustrated tears singeing the backs of her eyes.

Their heads were close, their breaths mingled. She slipped her hand around his neck and tugged. His hands slid to her waist and rested there.

The air between them charged. Time hung, suspended, as they searched each other's faces. The attraction between them almost sizzled.

Her fingers tingled, and she wanted nothing more than to tilt her head and press her lips to his. But she was his mentor. She had her children to consider. Like he read her decision on her face, his hands slipped away and he stepped back. If he would have leaned forward, she couldn't say she wouldn't have met him halfway. But his movement precluded her own.

She turned, her hand falling from his neck, the soft hair at his nape slipping through her fingers. Blindly, she grabbed the cream and turned toward the fridge, more to give herself something to do, to keep herself occupied until she had her rioting emotions back under control.

Grabbing the sugar, she put that away too.

After slapping the cupboard closed, she turned to him. He'd walked to the door and had his hand on the knob.

"What did you come here for? You said you wanted to talk." She sounded waspish and hated that, but she didn't know what to do about it.

His lips flattened. "Buy yourself a house. A nice one. The kind you deserve. Same with a car. BMWs have the highest safety ratings in crashes. Hire a nanny. And stop working so freaking much."

"You don't have the right to come in here and tell me what to do." The words flew out of her mouth, clearly enunciated, and hit him like hail on a roof.

"I just did."

She shoved her tender feelings down deep. "Take your opinions and leave."

"They'll let you keep the kids. If you have a house and some help and don't look like you're going to fall asleep on your feet."

Drat him. He knew her weakness. "No. The only way they'll let me keep the kids is if I have a husband or the strong potential for one."

"You've never had a problem finding boys who would fall all over themselves to spend just a few minutes in your presence." His expression seemed self-derisive, almost. Like he had been one of those boys.

But he never had.

She rolled her eyes. "You make that sound simple."

"I'm saying you have the pick of the litter. So pick."

She ran her eyes over his face, older, harder, but still the same. How could she tell him that she'd rather have no one if she could never have him? She looked away, running her finger over the edge of the counter.

He walked forward and leaned over the other side. "I'm out, Cassidy. Free. You can stop punishing yourself. And Jamal. And Nissa and Nessa. You do realize that you're punishing them now too, right?"

She hadn't thought about it, and it was one more thing for her to feel guilty about. She could have been giving her kids so much more—a nice house, a meal service, a housekeeper at the very least. She was the freaking pickle heiress. She had more money in her trust fund than she could ever use.

"Take the money from your trust fund—you still have your trust fund?" Torque's eyes narrowed, and she wished that she hadn't told him so much about her life back when they had slipped out together. He hadn't forgotten one detail.

She nodded.

"Buy a house. And a car. Hire a nanny. Cut your hours back to part-time, and relax with your kids for a while." He stared at her for a full minute before he turned and opened the door.

"That's not what you came here to talk to me about."

"No. It's not." The door clicked closed behind him.

Chapter 10

The next morning, Torque was at Tough's garage before the sun was up. He had struggled all night, trying to figure out how he could help Cassidy. After spending the evening with her, it was obvious she loved those precious children who needed a mom. Since he'd grown up without a dad, it tore at his heart to see those kids not have one either.

But the adoption board would never consider an ex-con who hadn't been on the outside for even a month as a suitable father. Plus, he didn't have a real job, and he'd never mentioned the money to Cassidy yesterday. He knew she had money. She'd mentioned her trust fund and the monthly stipend she received from the family business, even though she wasn't involved. It was time she spent it on herself and her kids. His pride wouldn't let him even ask about a loan. Not after seeing how she'd lived for the last ten years.

His pride also wouldn't let him tell her the only thing he wanted from her. It wasn't in payment for what he'd done, anyway.

A man's pride could sure be a pain in the butt sometimes.

There was a way he could kick some of his pride under the bus.

So, he'd walked to Tough's early.

Lights were on in the shop and the main door was unlocked, although the overhead garage doors were still closed.

Torque walked in to the smell of coffee and the sound of two old men arguing. Something about an article in the morning paper, apparently, since one of the old men by the checkerboard in the corner slapped the paper for emphasis while he insisted that the woman in the article was indeed the former mayor's daughter.

"Mr. Sigel, that is not the former mayor's daughter. He only had sons. Three sons. One of them married that Prichard girl. She wasn't much of a looker, but she always won the chocolate cake contest at the Ribbon Valley Farm Show. Quite a cook she was."

"That's where you're wrong, Al. First of all, the Prichard girl couldn't cook worth a fiddle-fart. She couldn't tell salt from sugar, and anyone who ever ate one of her sweet rolls can back me up on that."

Torque moved over to the coffeepot, figuring he might as well pour himself a cup while he was here. If this was what the old men did all morning, it wasn't any wonder that Tough was hiding somewhere, since the rest of the shop was deserted.

"Hey, now that must be the oldest brother." The men came up for air in their argument and realized Torque was there.

Black coffee in one hand, Torque strode over to the table and held out his other. "That's right. Torque, Tough's brother."

The one with the bushy eyebrows stood slowly to his feet and grabbed his hand first. "Name's Al. This here's Mr. Sigel."

The other man leaned heavily on his cane as he got to his feet, but Torque didn't insult him by offering to help. Once he stood, they shook. "Good to meet ya. You just came down from the state pen in Shartlesville, huh?"

Torque nodded.

"See Bobby Hamer there? He went up about fifteen years ago. Still there, far as I know."

Torque shook his head.

"Yeah. Probably don't do much socializing there."

A hand clamped on his back. Tough.

"Hey, man," Torque said. Tough had a brain that could put things together like nobody's business, but because he didn't talk much, especially at the beginning of a conversation—he didn't do much small talk—people often thought he was slow. The opposite was true. He also knew even though Tough looked like a ruffian, with his slightly shaggy hair sticking out from under his old ball cap, grease-stained t-shirt, old work jeans, and scuffed boots, Tough was probably about the most sensitive guy he knew and generous to a fault. Who else could put up with these old men all day every day?

Still, if anyone could help him with Cassidy, it'd be Tough.

Tough jerked his head in greeting. He was the only one of the four of them that didn't have a coffee in hand.

"'Morning," the old men greeted, and Tough nodded at them.

Torque eyed the old men. He hadn't wanted to make this a public discussion, and he was pretty sure the old-timers gossiped worse than a henhouse full of pullets, but that could work to his advantage.

He figured he might as well spit it out. Tough didn't do small talk anyway. "I have a unique favor, I thought you guys might be able to help me out."

"Shoot, boy," Mr. Sigel said.

Tough rested a hip on the side of the checker table and leveled the brown eyes they'd all inherited from their father at Torque.

"I know a lady. Classy woman. Works hard. Honest." He took a breath. How else to describe Cassidy? He could say she read his mind and spoke to his soul, but he wasn't doing this for himself. He hooked a hand around the back of his neck. "She's intelligent, strong, and independent. But she needs a husband. Fast."

"She fat?"

Mr. Sigel slapped his hand down on the paper. "Shut up, Al. That's not politically correct." He cracked his neck. "You say, 'is she pleasantly plump'?"

"That sounds like I'm describing a Thanksgiving turkey."

"It's better than what you said."

"Don't see why I can't just say what I mean."

"You don't want to be offensive." Al paused. "Not any more than you already are."

"Fine." He turned back to Torque. "Is she built like a linebacker or like the punter?"

"Ya can't say that either. That's discrimination against linebackers."

"I'm not discriminatin' against anyone. I'm just trying to find out what size the dad-blasted woman is."

"Then you say," Mr. Sigel said slowly like it was perfectly obvious, "'Is the enormity of her extensiveness on the weighing machine in proportion with the extensive magnitude of the magnificence of her cognitive vast immensity.'"

Torque blinked, trying to figure out what in the frig Mr. Sigel had just said.

A Jake brake filled the silence that descended.

"Turbo's here," Al announced.

Torque almost rolled his eyes. "Doesn't he realize people are still sleeping?"

"Ain't too many people around here that care," Mr. Sigel said.

Probably true. It was a bad area. Most folks had just gone to bed, and even a noise as loud as Turbo's Jake wouldn't wake them. Still.

The door opened. Turbo always blew in like a hurricane. "Man, Tough. You're letting ex-cons hang out here now?"

"Shut up, Turd," Torque said, using the old nickname from their childhood.

"Oh, that hurts." Turbo strode right over to the coffee maker and poured cream into a cup. He topped it off with a bit—a tiny bit—of coffee. "It's not my fault the old man saddled me with a name like Turbo. You don't have to make fun of it. My own brother. I took enough crap in school." He downed the cup of cream and poured another.

"That your breakfast?" Torque asked.

Turbo finished off the second cup and poured a third. "I think I forgot to eat yesterday."

Torque snorted. The big brother in him gaged Turbo's thin waist, although his shoulders, as well as Tough's, had filled out too, while he'd been in prison.

"Turbo, care to tell Al here that you can't say 'fat' and 'woman' in the same sentence?" Mr. Sigel asked, somewhat self-righteously.

"I didn't say that!" Al declared. "I said 'is she fat.'" His bushy brows lowered. "That's okay, isn't it, Turbo?"

Turbo lifted a shoulder. "If you're talking about a motorcycle."

"That's Fat Boy," Torque felt compelled to point out.

"Whatever." Turbo drained the third cup. "My opinion is: don't say the 'F' word."

"That meant something else when I was your age," Al muttered.

"*That* word's okay. But I wouldn't say 'fat' and 'woman' in the same decade. 'Less you're looking to get clobbered with someone's walker." Turbo smashed his Styrofoam cup and threw it in the trash. "Who ya calling fat, anyway?"

Mr. Sigel set the paper aside and started setting up the checkers. "Don't know. Torque's here looking for a husband for some chick, but he won't tell us what she looks like."

"I told you the important stuff."

"Like how much money she has?" Turbo hooked a hand around the lift hanging from the ceiling. "Repeat that info, please. I might be looking to get married."

Torque did roll his eyes at that. "She wouldn't put up with you for two seconds."

"You mean she couldn't catch me. Tell me how much money she has. I might slow down a little."

"You touch her, and you'll need a chair lift to get in and out of your truck."

"Okay. So, Turbo's out for a husband. If your own brother ain't good enough, who is?" Mr. Sigel scratched his mostly bald head.

"I don't know. That's why I'm here asking you."

"You want a man for Cassidy?" Tough finally spoke.

All eyes turned to him.

"Yeah," Torque said.

Turbo's mouth formed an "O" then snapped shut.

"Cassidy, the pickle heiress?" Al asked.

"No, you idiot," Mr. Sigel said, like he even knew.

"Oh. Must be Cassidy, the naked woman on all the billboards."

"You can't say 'naked.'" Mr. Sigel shook his finger at Al.

"What? That ain't politically correct either?"

"No. She ain't technically naked. You're being judgmental."

"Hain't judgmental. When I was your age, that was naked."

"I'm thinking not." Turbo smirked. "She's got the important bits covered, and you guys figured out how to make babies somehow."

"My wife wore a heck of a lot more than that when we 'made babies.' Long white nighty, and I only lifted it up to…"

"Stop right there." Holy frig. Torque didn't want to live with the image of Al in bed with his wife in his head for the rest of his life.

Mr. Sigel stroked his long nose. "This is Cassidy, the public defender who drives an old beater, lives in that rundown old apartment, and has the little boy with dark skin?"

"Yeah." *And* Cassidy, the pickle heiress.

"Whoo-hoo. Good luck with that. She's a sharp one. Gonna take three men and an elephant to tie her down." Al slapped the paper with a sharp crack, almost knocking his coffee cup over.

"You," Tough said.

Torque shook his head and put his hand up in a "stop" gesture. "Won't work. The adoption agency won't let her adopt the twins if she's not married or close to it, and the stink of prison is all over my sorry butt. No way they're going to accept me."

Tough slapped his arm. "Ain't no man for her but you."

Chapter 11

Tough turned and walked toward the four-door sedan parked in the far bay with the bumper and headlight torn off it.

Torque shoved his hands in his pockets and watched him go, not really seeing him but thinking about what he said. How had Tough come to that conclusion? No one, not even his brothers, knew what actually happened that night. He hadn't thought anyone knew about Cassidy and him that summer, either. She hadn't gone to his school. She graduated from an exclusive private girls' school a half an hour away. So they'd never even walked the halls together.

They'd not dated. They never even went out in public together. Her parents' mansion just happened to be over the low mountain from his gram's trailer park. Twenty minutes by car, going on the road. One mile as the crow flies. Fifteen minutes if a lonely boy were walking in the woods, wishing he had enough money to buy himself a gun and go hunting. Half that if a smart, independent, lonely girl were walking toward him from the opposite side.

They never planned to meet, and they only met in the woods a few times before she graduated high school. That was two years before him. She went to California to school. He didn't see her at all the first year she left. That year he started working at the garage full-time after being approved for the work-study program at school.

The next summer, she was back, rumored to have a big modeling contract. He ran into her several times around town, gorgeous, sophisticated. It wasn't hard to believe she was headed for the big time.

The end of that June, Cassidy's face showed up on insurance billboards across the state. At the same time, someone ripped a page out of a major brand sporting goods magazine with Cassidy modeling long underwear and tacked it to the post office bulletin board.

It was a restless summer for him. Probably typical teenaged boy hormones, fueled by being half in love with a girl who'd rocketed out of his orbit, as if she'd ever really been in it to begin with, considering where she came from and that he came from somewhere almost directly opposite of the pampered richness that defined her life.

He did some truck pulling for the garage he worked for. It was something he loved and kept him distracted.

He'd worked almost day and night on his pickup truck and finished it mid-June. Sometimes he'd slip out of the trailer at night, not really sneaking around because all he did was drive. But he'd spend hours with the windows down and the radio on, riding up and down the back roads. Dreaming, he supposed, but not really, since it wasn't even a good dream to think of Cassidy and him together. Too impossible.

First and only thing he'd ever stolen was the picture from the post office. It lay in his glove box as he wound around the back roads.

The Fourth of July was always a huge event in their town—carnival, games, contests, and, of course, fireworks at ten. It was a chance to see all the kids from school and see how everyone's summer was going. Typically, he loved it, but even though he'd heard about the fashion show they'd instigated in honor of the town's own fashion model, he didn't go.

He worked alone at the trailer on his pickup. His gram and brothers spent most of the day in town. Figured he'd at least go in for the fireworks, but he didn't feel like socializing. Although he considered taking his truck and parking somewhere along the road, that was an idea lots of other people always had, so he grabbed a flashlight and headed up the mountain to watch them from there.

He wasn't expecting Cassidy to be there, not with the fashion show. He wasn't under the pine tree where they'd met before anyway, since the view of the sky was blocked there. He was about a hundred yards away on a rocky outcropping. After deciding it would provide a great view of the fireworks, his other main thought had been that he hoped there were no snakes sharing his perch.

Too restless to sit, he'd stood for a while, one boot propped on a rock, his arm braced on his leg, watching the stars appear. Couldn't see the town, but it was down there. So was she. The thought made his heart hurt.

He heard her footsteps first, and he pulled his pocketknife out, thinking it was some kind of wild animal.

"Mind if I join you?" she asked, and his heart bowed down in homage.

They hadn't talked much, hadn't touched at all. But that was when she commented on his truck. He'd been proud as all get-out that she'd even noticed it and didn't hesitate to say yes when she asked about a ride. Which is when his slipping out at night became sneaking out.

Maybe Tough had heard him leave the house at night. But he couldn't have known he was meeting Cassidy. He'd only done it four Saturdays, sleeping through the Sunday sermons the next day, before she'd left town for a modeling gig she had before her semester started in mid-August.

The next time he'd seen her was the October Saturday after Homecoming. He didn't sleep through that Sunday's sermon.

He'd been in jail.

Chapter 12

Cassidy collapsed into the chair behind her desk. It had taken longer than she expected to meet with her newest assignment, but she still had fifteen minutes of her lunch break left, and she was going to do her part for Torque in the sponsorship program if she could.

Punching up the websites that she'd found on her phone late last night, she initiated the call to the first one: Pete's Towing and Recovery.

"Hello, Pete's," a rough male voice answered.

Cassidy cleared her throat. "Hello. This is Cassidy Kimball. I'm an attorney in Brickly Springs. I have a diesel mechanic who's been in a bit of a rough spot and needs work. I will vouch for him completely. Do you think you could help me out?"

"He needs a job?"

"Either that, or he could do any work that you might be too busy to squeeze in."

"What's his name?"

"Torque Baxter."

There was silence on the end of the phone. "Torque Baxter. Heck yeah. Give me his number. I didn't know he was back in town."

"Just a couple of days ago," Cassidy said, tapping her pen on her desk. "I actually don't know his number, but I'll get it to you as soon as I can. In the meantime, I know his brothers can get ahold of him." She rattled off the numbers she'd written down earlier that she'd gotten when she'd called Torque's gram on the way in to the office that morning.

"Thanks a lot, Miss Kimball."

Cassidy thanked him and hung up. She'd initiated the call, but that guy was thrilled to hear about Torque. She kind of figured it would be that way.

Smiling to herself, she pulled up the next website and dialed the number.

TOUGH GAVE TORQUE A ride from his garage to the other side of town and Mrs. Ford's place. He had a week. Coming up with the money was pretty much out of the question, but he could still hang out at the garage for a while. Maybe something would work out.

He'd gone through all the tools, handling them, remembering, taking stock of where they were kept. It was well-organized, and there was very little he would change.

By noon, he was in the office, looking through the account books.

A tap on the open office door startled him. "You Torque Baxter?"

Torque looked up into the crinkled blue eyes of a fellow in his fifties. He wore a button-up shirt that hung over his protruding belly, loose jeans. A chain, probably hooked to his wallet, hung down almost to his knees.

"Yeah."

"Heard you were back in town. Name's John." He walked forward with his hand out. "Are you open for business, or what?"

Torque stood behind the desk and shook. "Depends on what you need."

"Uh, okay. Not sure. I've got this vibration in my steering wheel. Had it for a while, but it got worse this morning. Called a couple different garages, and the earliest they can get me in is next week. 'Fraid she's not going to last until then."

Torque tried to still the jumping excitement in his chest. He kept his voice steady. "Make and model?"

"359 Pete."

Nice. An old truck. "I can figure out what the problem is. Can't guarantee I can fix it here. I don't have any accounts set up, and I'm limited on parts." He came around the desk. "Let's see what it is first, then we'll worry about how we'll get it fixed."

John shuffled his feet. "That's great. I don't want to lose any more work than I have to, and I definitely don't want to break down along the road."

Torque found the broken U-bolt right away. After digging around, he found one in the garage, so he made a note that he was using it—if he wasn't able to come up with the money to rent the place, he was definitely going to pay back all the parts he used—jacked the frame up to remove the old one, and stuck the new one on.

By two o' clock, John was gone. A check for the U-bolt and for two hours of shop rate labor lay in the top desk drawer in the office.

Torque looked around. He'd seen Mrs. Ford when he was in the shop a while ago, but she'd disappeared since he'd walked into the office and settled up with John. He headed into the garage and waited for his eyes to get used to the dimmer lighting.

She sat on a chair over in the far corner. Her hands were moving... Torque squinted then strolled over. "Hey."

She looked up. "Oh? John's gone. Were you able to fix his truck?"

"Yeah." He hesitated before adding, "It was a U-bolt."

"Oh. Not a big deal then," she said.

Hmm. So, maybe she knew a little something about trucks. Made sense since her husband had a garage.

Her hands dropped to her lap, and her brows knotted. "Do you mind if I sit here? I'm not checking up on you, but after the girls moved out, I often brought my quilting down to the garage. I kept Tyke company, and he kept me company." Her lip trembled slightly. "I can go back to the house if I make you nervous."

"Love it." He did. After his mom died, it felt like the hole she left in his heart never completely healed. Mrs. Ford would never be his mom, but her presence felt like salve over his wound. "If I stay, I'll get you a table and a more comfortable chair."

Her eyes filled up, and her smile trembled. "Thank you."

He nodded. "Thank you for giving me this week."

She looked down at her hands holding the material in her lap. Her voice came out soft. "Do you think you'll stay?"

He took a breath, wanting with every fiber of his being to be able to say yes, but he had to be honest. "Not sure how I'm going to pull it together."

She nodded. She'd been the wife of a business owner long enough that she surely knew hard decisions sometimes had to be made. The rumble of a truck interrupted his thoughts.

"Got company," he said.

"Got a customer," she corrected. "That's Tom's tow truck, or I didn't spend twenty years sitting in this garage listening to diesel motors."

He hardly thought that she could actually recognize Tom's truck, but when he walked out the door, it was Tom sitting in the big parking lot, hooked to a yellow Freightliner. He was climbing out of his truck, and Torque walked over. A small bit of excitement built in his chest, like sprouts pushing out of an acorn. Could this really be more work?

"Torque." Tom grinned as he walked over, slightly hunched as though his back bothered him.

They shook.

Tom lifted up his cap, shoving a calloused hand through his sparse hair. "Turbo called me a little bit ago. Said you's opening up shop here, and if I had any business I could direct your way, he'd appreciate it."

Torque's throat tightened. Turbo had never said a word. Gosh, it felt good to be back out where his brothers had his back. Before he'd gone up, Turbo had been a gangly teen, full of fun and pranks like skipping class to go roof-surfing past the school. He'd followed Torque around at the garage, always with a grin and a joke.

But this wasn't a joke.

"I happened to get a call today from the police. It'll be an insurance job."

Torque sighed inside. An estimate first. Good money if he got the job, but slow. It wouldn't save him. Still, he wasn't going to turn it down.

"I ain't forgot what you did for my boy."

Torque lifted a shoulder, brushing it off. "Wasn't anything."

"Was to him. You won that truck pull, took my boy down the track beside you for exhibition...you might not understand, but to someone like him, with that simple kind of mind...he sat in the passenger seat and waved. Thought it was the best thing ever. Believe it or not, he still talks about it."

He'd had the option of taking Cassidy, since she was the fair queen, but he'd opted for the boy with Down's syndrome. It was safer. Cassidy? Well, he'd seen her later that night. Alone. "I'm far from building a pulling truck, but he's welcome here at the shop, as long as I'm here."

"We'll see. Maybe some Saturday. He's got a program he's in, lets him work a job that's not too hard for him to handle. Boy does good." He slapped his leg.

"Good." Torque didn't add that he might not be here. Might as well act like it was his. Maybe someday it would be. "'Preciate the business."

"Ya need to get a phone."

As soon as he could afford it. "It's on my list."

"You can charge yard fee on this truck too. Going rate's anywhere from two hundred to five hundred a day."

He hadn't considered that, and he thanked Tom for reminding him.

Tom backed the truck into the garage and left.

At eight o' clock that evening, Torque wiped his hands on a rag, feeling much better about his business than he had to start the day. He walked over to where Mrs. Ford, no, Miss Angelina—she'd insisted he call her that—was putting her quilting away.

"Word has sure gotten around," she said with crinkled eyes and a big smile.

"Yeah." For the hundredth time that day, he made a mental note to thank Tough who had sent a diesel pickup over and also a T Tag dump, both of which had stopped at his place to get worked on, but he didn't handle diesels, and the dump was bigger than what he normally handled.

Torque also needed to thank Turbo who had apparently used his CB to tell everyone he passed that day that Torque Baxter was back in town. He needed to get his inspection license, since he'd turned two people away for that. He also needed to get a phone.

Miss Angelina tucked the piece she'd been working on into her bag and stood to go.

"I'll drive up to the house with you then walk back down and lock up."

Miss Angelina walked over to Torque, reached one hand up, and patted his cheek. "Thank you, son. This is almost like my Tyke was still alive."

"I'm the one that needs to be thanking you. I don't deserve this opportunity, but I'm grateful for it. Just hope it works out."

"If it's meant to be, it will."

He drove her up, parked her buggy, and made sure she got into the house okay, declining her offer of a late supper. After walking back down, he went inside the garage, checking to make sure everything was away for the night. He'd not been entrusted with this much responsibility for a long time.

His back hurt, and so did his feet. But he was wearing work boots and his own clothes, even if they were too small. His hands were dirty, and he'd spent the day in good, honest labor. He felt like a man again. It was a feeling he wouldn't take for granted.

He also felt optimistic for the first time in ages. So long, he'd almost forgotten what it felt like—eagerness to get going on the next day. Excitement. The feeling of having a productive place in the world.

And, man...his brothers. They'd come through for him in a big way today. Neither one of them was completely normal. How could they be after their childhood? Felt good to be part of a family again.

He closed the door, pocketing the key. The only thing that could possibly make anything better would be if he were going home to his wife and children.

GRAM SAT AT THE KITCHEN table with an electronic tablet in front of her. Torque stopped and did a double take. His gram looked up over her glasses. "What? Ain't used to an old lady that knows how to use the newfangled electronic gadgets?"

"Guess not." Torque sat on the bench by the door and unlaced his boots. "I didn't know you were into stuff like that."

"Wasn't." She shrugged. "Cassidy Kimball convinced me to try it out." Her wise blue eyes watched him shrewdly. "I wasn't the quickest learner, but she came over a bunch until I got the hang of it. Kinda thought like she was in cahoots with Tough and Turbo taking her turn watching me, but I did learn how to work the thing well enough that I can read my Bible in big print and get the latest ladies' Bible studies up. I order my groceries on it sometimes, too."

Torque nodded, toeing off his second boot and setting them neatly under the bench. Turbo and Tough both had their own homes, but while he'd been gone, they'd taken turns caring for Gram. Apparently, Cassidy had helped.

A new and somewhat surprising picture of Cassidy was emerging in his head.

"Seems like since you went to prison, that girl's been Dolly Do-Gooder. Any idea why?" Gram closed the cover on her tablet and set it aside.

Cassidy had said something about paying, hadn't she?

"But I think she's finally bitten off more than she can chew with those kids. Hard enough to raise kids with a husband in the picture." Gram shook her head and reached into the cupboard to get a bowl out.

"I can heat up my own supper. Relax, Gram." He tried to take the bowl from her.

"Sit, boy." She pulled the bowl away from him. "I ain't too old and decrepit to feed my grandson. Take it easy." She scooped some vegetable soup into his bowl.

Torque's mouth watered. Gram called it vegetable soup, but she always put a whole roast in with the veggies. Whatever spices and anything else she put in combined to make it taste amazing. It smelled amazing. They sure didn't make stuff like this in prison.

She put the bowl in the microwave and pushed the buttons.

"In fact..." His gram turned and looked at him with that look he remembered well from childhood. She had a plan brewing behind her ice blue eyes, and he wasn't going to like it. "In fact, I think once you eat, you and me ought to walk over to her apartment, and you can take her out for some ice cream. I owe her for all the help she gave me on that there electric thingy." Gram nodded at her tablet.

"You owe her? So I pay her?"

"Yep."

"With ice cream?"

"Don't know too many girls that would turn down ice cream."

Twenty minutes and a nice, leisurely stroll later, Torque knocked on Cassidy's door. Gram hadn't chatted much on the way over, and he'd had time to think. He'd told Cassidy to take it easy, get a new apartment, and a bunch of other things. Bossed her. But not helped her. Well, taking her out, even if it was just for ice cream, would get her away a little. Regardless, she needed support more than she needed him telling her what to do.

Gram stood beside him, impatiently tapping her cane on the ground. She didn't really need the cane, but Turbo and Tough had cajoled and pleaded until she used it. Most of the time.

His hand was raised to knock again when the door opened and Cassidy stood outlined against the light, wearing soft, old jeans and a sweatshirt with the cuffs and neck frayed and the wording faded to unreadability.

Her eyes widened. His heart thundered. He took a breath to speak, but as was usual, Gram spoke first.

"Put shoes on. I told you I'd pay you back for helping me with that electronic thing, and Betty down at the post office has been telling me you're needing a break. I'm sitting with the kids, and Torque's treating you to ice cream."

Cassidy stood statue-still, her hand still on the doorknob. Her spine straightened, and her chin came up.

Torque sighed silently. Sometimes Gram was a little much. Grown people didn't appreciate being bossed around. Cassidy probably wanted to be ordered to take a break and get ice cream just as much as he wanted to show up at his gram's side like an obedient dog.

But he'd been gone too long and not home long enough to have the will to fight his gram.

Cassidy, however, deserved better. He stepped forward, glad he'd insisted he needed to shower before showing up at her door. "I'm sorry I didn't call. I—" He paused, realizing suddenly that he'd never asked a girl on a date before. Even an ice-cream date. He felt like a twelve-year-old with his gram standing beside him. His stomach tightened like a rusty motor with no oil. "I'd like to buy you ice cream." Flashes of late-night rides, midnight air, and a big, fat moon shimmering on the horizon tore through his head. Exotic fruit scented it all. Standing here in the hall, he could breath it in, full and deep. "Walk with me for a bit?"

She swallowed. Her eyes closed, and her hand gripped the door. Then the starch came back, and her head bent regally, somehow making him feel like she was looking down rather than up. "I'd love to," she said.

Her voice trembled ever so slightly, and he wondered which signal was the true Cassidy. The regal air? Or the vulnerable insecurity?

"Come in for a minute while I throw shoes on." She opened the door farther, and Torque followed his gram in, pushing the door shut behind them.

He leaned a shoulder against the doorjamb while Cassidy rattled off instructions to Gram, even though the kids were all in bed. She pulled on worn, brown cowgirl boots with blunt toes. Torque didn't bother to try to look away. Her graceful movement, her slim hips and the soft curve of her waist, her long, shiny hair which hung down her back in soft waves—he had dreamed about it all in prison. She was here now, standing in front of him, and he wasn't going to deny himself the pleasure of looking.

"I got it. I have your number, and I'll call you if anything comes up. It's not like he's taking you to France." Gram waved them off.

Torque opened the door. Cassidy's hand hovered above her purse.

"You don't need it." Torque held the door.

She gave him a tight smile. Was she nervous? Finally, she left the purse on the counter, pushing her phone into her back pocket, and walked out the door ahead of him.

He caught his gram giving him a shrewd look as he closed the door. Maybe Gram had ulterior motives for what she'd done tonight. Probably. Gram wasn't slow. But he wasn't sure what her thoughts were. He just knew his. He wanted Cassidy to have a good time. With him.

Chapter 13

Cassidy walked down the stairs in front of Torque. What was up with him just showing up? She couldn't stop her heart from beating happily, but her head knew it wasn't because he'd all the sudden decided that they were meant for each other.

He'd almost kissed her, then he'd walked away. After telling her everything that was wrong with her life, first, of course. She should be angry. Only, he was right.

He opened the outside door, and she stepped out onto the sidewalk. She turned and faced him. "You were right."

His feet planted. "About what?"

She put her hands on her hips and tilted her head. "I wasn't being fair to my kids. You're out and free. I feel like I still owe you, but I need to stop making decisions based on whether or not I can enjoy my life."

His jaw tightened. "You don't owe me." He looked out over the parking lot. In a tight t-shirt, his shoulders seemed extra broad. "I don't want to make anything harder for you, but there's nothing you can do to get those years back for me. It's over. I didn't do it thinking that you were going to pay me."

"Then why?"

He touched her arm. "Let's walk." His hand slid down the sensitive skin on her forearm, past her wrist. Their fingers tangled and held. She breathed in the early fall air. Warm and slightly scented with the spicy smell of falling leaves and resting earth. Torque's male scent, that one that was all his own, pushed the old memories of happier times and hot summer nights closer to the front of her mind.

"I'm not used to walking with you."

"Yeah. We can drive if you want, but we'll have to take your car."

"I miss your old truck."

He was quiet for a few steps. "Guess that's the least of the things that were lost that night."

It was on the tip of her tongue to apologize again, but he seemed irritated when she did and she couldn't blame him. Apologies didn't do any good. That's why she'd made sure her actions counted.

"We don't have to be serious tonight, do we?" he asked softly.

What was it like to not be serious? She couldn't even remember. With law school, then her job, plus working to secure the mentorship program—it was a good program, but she did have an ulterior motive—now with the kids.

"I'm not sure I remember how."

Torque changed direction, pulling her with him. "Maybe I can remind you."

They were headed out of town. "Where...?"

He laughed. "It's pretty warm out tonight..."

"No!" She laughed. "You are not getting me to go swimming."

"Not swimming." He laughed with her and swung their linked hands between them.

A weight she didn't even know she'd been carrying lifted off her chest. "The only thing this way is a few old houses, an abandoned warehouse, and the rail line that only has coal trains once a week. I'm not playing chicken, even if this was the train night, which I don't think it is."

"There's a creek down here."

"You already said we weren't swimming. It's not that warm." A soft breeze riffled through the leaves of the maples above them, making a sandpaper sound and causing several leaves to drift down through the last streetlight by the gas station before they left the town limits.

"Not swimming. But there used to be a rope down here, under the railroad bridge that goes over the creek."

"There was?"

"Rich ticks swam in their backyard pools. Us poor boys used the creek."

Her chest constricted. "I'm sorry."

"Shut up. Smile." His words were blunt, but he said them in the same tone of voice he might have said "I love you, Cassidy" in, and her chest loosened, but her heart flipped a little crazily. He brought her hand to his mouth and touched his lips to it softly.

"There was a rope under the bridge. We used to swing on it and do flips into the water. We'd try to make it the whole way across the creek, too. It's not that deep, so you couldn't dive in." They came to a gate in the fence, and he pushed against the chain while she bent and slipped through. "It's a good thing I picked a skinny girl."

"Humph." She put her hands on her hips and regarded him through the fence. "And you've brought how many girls through here?"

He stopped in the act of bending down. His face lifted, and his smile faded. "I've never taken another girl anywhere."

They stared at one another. Cassidy's neck tingled, and her heart thumped. Of course he hadn't. He'd only been seventeen when he was arrested. But his eyes were deep and dark and seemed to say it was so much more than just having the opportunity.

He shook his head and grinned, like he had remembered that they were going to have fun. Because things had definitely felt like they were getting serious.

"Are we trespassing here?"

"Yep." Torque groaned as he tried to slide his chest through the gap in the gate. It stuck. "I didn't have this much trouble ten years ago."

"I don't think you're going to make it."

"I think you're right," he said as he stood.

She moved back to the gate, intending to slide back through. "I guess I should have brought a skinny guy."

He laughed. "I deserved that." He put a hand up. "Hold it."

She stopped.

WHAT HE WANTS

He backed up three steps then rushed the gate, taking two giant steps up, gripping with his hands, before kicking his legs to the side and swinging over. He landed with a thump, sinking down into a crouch before standing up in front of her. It was an impressive display.

"So, you're coming down here to show off?" she asked with a jaunty tilt to her head. No point in letting him know her heart had just kicked up three gears.

"You know how many times I sat and stared at the prison fence and wished I could just jump over it and walk away?"

Her face felt like it was melting.

He saw it immediately. He reached out and bumped her shoulder with his hand. "Pretty spectacular, wasn't it?" His teeth flashed in the moonlight.

Forcing herself to grin, she said, "Bet you can't do it again."

He laughed, grabbing her hand and walking to the railroad tracks.

"So, now I suppose you're going to show off on the rope, too?" She pushed aside the weights and the old feelings of guilt and duty that threatened to ruin their time and instead concentrated on just enjoying the banter and friendship of the man beside her.

"Nah. I'm not buying you ice cream unless you make it across."

"Seriously? I have to earn my ice cream?"

"Yep. You've freeloaded long enough."

He was making fun of her. She laughed. The lawyer in her wanted to take the opposite side, which was the side that he'd been arguing—that she wasn't a freeloader and didn't have to "earn" anything.

"That was good," she finally said, with more than a little admiration at his ability to see what she was doing and turn it on its head.

"Hey, being a mechanic is a lot of hard work, but your mind is often free to wander. Occasionally I come up with something good." His hand tightened on hers. "The bridge is right there. That's what those metal rails are."

The moonlight glinted off the place where he pointed.

"The trail is over here." He pulled her to his side and stepped off the railroad track. "I'll go first."

"That's what I was thinking."

He snorted. "Put a hand on my shoulder to balance."

She obeyed, his shoulder hard and strong under her hand, and followed him carefully down the steep bank. Her eyes were adjusted to the dark, and the moon gave enough light to make out shapes. The gurgle of the stream and the rattle of the leaves overhead gave the impression of cheerfulness despite the darkness. Cassidy's heart felt light. She hummed softly to herself.

"Good song." Torque stopped at the bottom of the bank and turned left toward the underside of the bridge.

She stopped humming, realizing she'd been singing an old hymn in her head.

"Don't quit," he said low.

She used to sing to the radio. Sometimes Torque would join in, his bass blending with her alto. She'd forgotten.

"It's still there," Torque said. "Or someone hung a new one."

"How will we know?"

"I'll test it out first."

She reached in her pocket for her phone and pulled up the flashlight app, handing it to Torque.

"Yeah, definitely a new one," he said as he looked up. He handed her phone back. "You might want to put that on the ground somewhere, just in case."

"I'm not getting wet."

"So, if I fall in, you're not coming in to rescue me?"

"You can't swim?"

His teeth flashed. "Maybe."

"How are you getting it?" The rope looked to be just out of arm's reach.

He looked around before picking up a good-sized stick, using it to hook the rope and bring it to him. "Like that."

He climbed up on a big rock that she hadn't noticed. "The trick to getting the whole way across is getting up high and back as far as you can."

"Okay." She was not going to swing on the rope but figured now wasn't the time to argue.

"Here I go." He jumped back and kicked his feet up, flying across the creek. Cassidy body tensed. Maybe they should have checked to make sure the other side was safe.

With a crash, a thump, and a triumphant hoot, he landed. "Catch the rope," he called.

She stumbled but managed to grab it as it swung to her.

"Now you."

"No way."

He put his hands on his hips. "Really?"

"I might not be able to hold on the whole way."

"So you'll drop into the creek. Not a big deal."

"It could hurt."

"Okay. Throw the rope over here."

She did, and he swung back. "It's always easier to swing from that side to this one because it's higher."

"I see."

"Okay, up you go." He grabbed her hand and tugged. She pulled back.

He gave her hand a slight jerk, and she fell into his chest. One arm came around her. The other held onto the rope.

"Stop being a grown-up."

She choked out a laugh. His chest was solid and strong and warm under his soft tee. And his arm felt like steel, clamping her tight, making her feel anchored and secure. She really had promised to let go, to not be serious. He'd said even if she fell she wouldn't get hurt...

"Don't do it for me. Do it for ice cream." His voice was light and teasing, despite the hard and fast thumping of his heart under her cheek.

"Okay. For ice cream."

"Yes!" He did a slight fist pump with the hand that held the rope. "Up you go." He lifted her up on the rock. "Hold on," he said, climbing on behind her.

He stood behind her, his arms around her holding onto the rope. "Grab ahold. I'm going to jump back, then my body will be under yours. Stick your feet straight out if you can, like you're on a swing."

How many years had it been since she'd been on a swing? A long time. And never a swing like this, with Torque's solid body behind her. The heat sizzled through the layers of clothes. His biceps bulged on either side of her face, and his strong hands held the rope just above hers.

"Okay." She took a deep breath. More to calm the attraction that made her want to push back into him than to calm any nerves. If there was one thing Torque had proven over the years, it was that Torque would protect her no matter what it cost him.

"Counting to three...one...two...three!" He jumped, and Cassidy jumped back with him, picking her feet up and sticking them out.

The freedom of flying, intensified by the darkness which heightened her other senses—the babbling of the creek, the wind on her face, Torque's heat behind her, his breath in her ear, his heart thumping, strong and true, against her back—gave her a feeling of weightlessness and complete abandon. She screamed in pure joy.

Suddenly the tension in the rope disappeared. Torque scrambled behind her. She panicked, stiffening.

"Grab my neck!" Torque's body shifted in midair, and she twisted, feeling for his neck and gripping it with her arms.

An abrupt stop and a splash. Cold water splashed her face and arms, but Torque had his arms around her back and knees, holding her like a baby, and she stayed out of the water.

He stumbled. "Uff." His hands tightened. She gripped his neck, the rumbling water close enough to feel the cooler air at its surface.

Torque's breath blew on her face as he steadied himself on one knee, the other supported her back. A giggle bubbled just under her collarbone.

"Are you okay?" His voice whispered across her face, and she shivered.

"I'm fine," she said. "You're wet. Are you hurt?"

"I'm glad I'm wet. I wouldn't want you to think I planned this." He stood to his feet, the water splashing around them. "Glad it's been a little dry this year and the creek's low. It would have softened the landing, but you'd have gotten wet if the water had been higher." He splashed out of the creek and set her down. She didn't let go of his neck right away, and they ended up pressed together, his hands on her hips.

"Why would I have thought you planned it?" she asked, a little breathlessly. Neither of them was hurt, and it had been fun, even after the rope broke. For her at least. She wasn't wet.

"So I could hold you." His hands tightened on her waist, and his head bent so his cheek rested against her temple so his words hit her ear then drove straight to her heart.

"You don't have to make up elaborate schemes with frayed ropes and water in order to hold me."

His body stiffened. His chest heaved in and out. It took him so long to answer that she wasn't sure he was going to. "This was almost as good as driving with you."

They could have been teenagers again, with no worries and few cares, driving down the back roads, free and easy.

"I miss your old pickup."

He stepped back, and she let her arms drop, missing his heat immediately. "I'd rather have gone driving, but I need to put a truck together first."

He grabbed her hand, and she laughed. "You're the only person I've ever met that doesn't 'buy' a truck, but 'puts one together.'"

His chuckle drifted back as he led her out from under the bridge. "I'd fall in that dang creek a hundred times to hear you laugh. You need to do it more often."

Her smile froze on her face. "It's good to hear you laugh too. It's actually good just to hear you at all." She didn't mean to slam him for not talking to her after he went to prison, but it had hurt. She'd thought she meant something to him, but he'd completely shut her out.

He paused, one foot on the bank, ready to climb up. "I'm sorry." He turned, searched her face.

"Why?" she asked, even though it wasn't the first time, and he'd refused to answer her.

She could hardly contain her surprise when he put a hand in his pocket and shifted, opening his mouth.

"I know you tried. And...just that one time you walked in, all the guys catcalling. You looked so good. And I..." He swallowed. "I couldn't stand it."

"Couldn't stand that I looked good?" Cassidy barely breathed. She'd wondered for so long why he'd treated her like a stranger, like she meant less than nothing to him. They hadn't been a couple, exactly. They hadn't dated. But they'd had *something*. Something real.

He shook his head. "No. Couldn't stand, first of all, that you were in that hellhole, around all those guys who weren't good enough to even look at you, because of me. But more than that, couldn't stand that I wasn't able to work to be worthy of you."

"That's crap," she interrupted. But he held his hand up.

"No. I was a poor boy with nothing. But at least I was able to be working to be something. To have something. Once I went up, it was gone, and I was less than nothing. It was selfish of me, but it was easier to not see you." He rubbed his thumb over her cheek and rested it next to her mouth. "To smell you, touch you. The one time you visited... Knowing I was nothing... It was torture. I took the easy way out and turned my back on you."

She shivered.

She didn't realize she was crying until his thumb brushed the wetness on her cheek.

"Serving the time, yeah, that was hard. But seeing you and not being able to have you? That was too hard."

"I would have waited. I *did* wait."

"I couldn't ask that of you."

Her neck heated. Her fingernails bit into her palms. "You were in prison for me! What do you mean you couldn't ask that of me?"

"Wasn't worth it. *I* wasn't worth it."

Her chest was too full for her to form words. She didn't even know what to say. Anger, sure, burnt up her throat. But he'd also admitted that he'd ignored her in prison, not because he hated her, which is what she'd thought, but because he wanted her so much. Her heart fluttered. Everything she'd done in the past ten years was with the thought of the man in front of her in mind. Everything. Which maybe made her a bad person, because she should do right because it was good. Not because she owed someone.

He didn't give her a chance to get her thoughts organized but grabbed her hand and pulled her up the bank.

"Come on. It's cold."

He was soaked from the waist down. Maybe he really was cold. Or maybe he was just done talking about it.

She didn't know what to say anyway, and he didn't seem to want to hear it, even if she did figure something out.

They walked in silence back to her apartment.

Chapter 14

"Thank you so much for meeting me at the park," Cassidy said to Elizabeth, the woman who was applying for her nanny position, as she pushed the twins on the baby swings.

Golden leaves overhead contrasted with an azure sky. The temperature was perfect autumn weather.

"It's not a problem. As a nanny, I'm familiar with parks." Elizabeth wore gray sneakers with black leggings and a long-sleeved t-shirt. Maybe not the nicest clothes to wear to an interview, but clothes that would be perfect for watching children.

"Great. Because I'll want them to spend as much time outside as possible." Cassidy went on, asking the questions she'd researched last night when she couldn't sleep after Torque had left. Early this morning, she had called off work. Torque was right—she didn't have anything to prove anymore. He was out.

She'd decided last night that she was making some serious changes.

She hadn't been expecting to have a candidate to interview so quickly, but the agency she'd gone through was one of the best. She'd checked out Elizabeth's references and read the agency's report. Everything looked excellent.

Elizabeth gave all the right answers. She also pushed one of the girls on the swing the whole time. Cassidy felt comfortable with her and optimistic when she left, after making arrangements for Elizabeth to watch the children that evening. Maybe finding a nanny wouldn't be as hard as she feared. Although there was still a part of her that hadn't accepted the fact that she couldn't do it all.

As the twins slept in the stroller, Cassidy made several phone calls, lining up her plans for tonight. A little excitement blinked inside of her. She couldn't remember the last time she'd had an evening with the girls.

"IT WAS HARDER TO LEAVE the kids with a new sitter than I thought it would be." Cassidy wiggled her nose, trying to itch it without touching it with her hands, which were mostly covered in bright green paint.

"They're fine. You checked out her references. She came highly recommended." Kelly stood on a ladder, rolling white paint on the old ceiling. This was her project, so she volunteered to do the hardest part. "I really appreciate you spending your girls' night helping me. The activity center is scheduled to open next week, and there's so much to do. But the ads have already gone out."

Harris's curly red hair bounced in its ponytail as she leaned around the doorframe, brushing cheerful yellow into the corners. "I think if it were me, I wouldn't let them with her for very long. In case something is wrong."

Cassidy dipped her roller in the paint tray. Harris was much more cautious than Kelly. Maybe to a fault. "I was thinking four hours. Do you think that's too much?" Wiping her hand on her loose, old jeans, she dug her phone out of her pocket. Eight o' clock. Two hours so far.

"We'll be done painting in fifteen minutes. You could go check then. We'll clean up." Kelly glanced at Harris who nodded.

"And if they're fine, you can come back and help with putting the hardwood floor down. We need to go rent the nail gun anyway."

Was she being too protective? She didn't think so. The twins were her responsibility. They'd already had so much neglect and confusion in their lives.

"I've heard part of being a mother is taking care of yourself. Stop worrying," Kelly said with an easy smile.

It reassured her, since Kelly had seen some awful things in her line of social work. If she wasn't concerned... They would be fine. Cassidy closed her eyes and took a deep breath.

"Have you seen Torque again?" Kelly climbed down the ladder and moved it forward a few feet before climbing back up to get at a new patch of ceiling.

"At the mentorship meeting."

She paused on the ladder steps. "How'd that go?"

"Good, I guess. He agreed to do it, anyway. But he really doesn't want my help."

"Why not?"

Kelly grinned and continued climbing. "Took one look at your beautiful face and decided he'd ditch the mentorship since he couldn't date you if you were doing that."

"Not likely." Cassidy used her arm to push a few stray hairs back from her face. "I think it's a pride thing."

"Men have a problem with it a lot of times." Harris moved her paintbrush thoughtfully.

"I'm not sure." They hadn't talked much. But she felt like he was the only person in the world who thought she was more than a pretty face. Still, the memory of their almost kiss, mixed with their pre-prison history, made her long to wish he really did want to ditch the mentorship so he could date her. It was what she always wanted anyway.

Kelly gave her a warning look. "I'd worry about him being around the kids before your new nanny."

"What crime did he commit? It wasn't one with kids, was it?" Harris asked.

"Of course not. Vehicular homicide was the charge." As always, guilt placed a heavy hand on the back of her neck when she talked like the charges were actually Torque's instead of hers. She'd never get used to making him take the blame.

"Was he drunk?" Harris asked softly.

The hand squeezed. Hard. She flinched. "No. But there was a bottle of vodka in the glove compartment. Half gone. And a bag of weed."

"Ugh. He sounds like a winner." Kelly made a face.

"They weren't his."

Kelly rolled her eyes. "That's what they all say."

"No. They really weren't." She'd put them there. She hadn't meant to, and Torque didn't know it. But she'd been carrying them with her that night after taking them from her mother. Why she hadn't just thrown the stuff away, she couldn't say. She certainly hadn't planned on stashing them in Torque's glove box. But she'd been snooping in his truck, curious about the boy who wasn't like the other boys she knew. She wanted to know him better. Well, she'd sure gotten a surprise when she'd opened his glove box and seen the picture that he kept in there.

Her.

He had a picture of her in his truck. Folded four ways, and worn, like he'd gotten it out a lot and looked at it.

She didn't even look that great—she was modeling long underwear and wore hiking boots—who even did that?

Honestly, the find had shocked her. At first, it made her think he was just like everyone else, looking at her like a pinup. It hurt. She'd been so sure he was different. That, combined with the fighting at home, and the news that her parents were splitting, plus her mother's drinking and drug issues...well, there would never be an excuse good enough for what she did next.

Kelly broke the silence. "We're waiting."

Cassidy looked around. Her roller was dripping on the particle board floor, while Kelly and Harris had stopped what they were doing and were staring at her.

"You sound like you know what you're talking about. Neither of us knew you back them. Well, I did, but not very well." Harris was several years younger than her.

"So spill." Kelly leaned over the top of the ladder, her roller still.

Cassidy swallowed. No one knew the truth. Torque wouldn't talk to her, and she didn't want to contradict his story. She'd never told a soul. Her heart started slamming in her chest, like it wanted to escape.

"I know he didn't, because I put them there."

"Why?" Harris asked.

"You and Torque Baxter?" Kelly almost fell off the ladder. The left side lifted off the floor before slamming back down.

"No way," Harris said.

"It wasn't like that."

"What was it like, then?"

Cassidy swallowed. "We knew each other. I rode around with him a few times in his truck." She lifted a shoulder. How to describe the feelings that she wasn't even sure about? In the end, she just couldn't. Whatever they'd had, she ruined, but it was still precious to her. And private. "I took the dope and drink from my mom, and it ended up in his truck. The cops found it after the accident."

"He never told them different?"

"No."

"You never came forward."

"No. He...he wanted to protect me, I think. He didn't dispute that it was his, and when I tried to talk to him, to tell him I needed to take the fall, he refused. I didn't want him to get nailed for giving false statements, and I really didn't have any proof that it was mine. My mom certainly wasn't going to back me up, so I let it go."

"Wow." Kelly's eyes were huge. "So he took the fall for the booze and dope."

"Yes." And for so much more.

"How did you pay him?"

"He wouldn't take anything. I tried to send him money in prison. He wouldn't touch it." She shouldn't have known, but as an attorney, she knew people who knew people, which was how the government worked.

"So you're helping him with the mentorship program."

"He really wouldn't take that either. He said he wanted to earn his living with his own hands. He wasn't going to let me be his mentor, which hasn't helped as much as I'd hoped."

"I don't understand why he wouldn't have denied knowing anything about the booze and drugs." Harris gave Cassidy a look. "There's more, isn't there?"

Cassidy bit her lip. Her legs shook, and she stumbled to a bucket of joint compound, slowly sinking down on it.

"Cassidy?" Kelly asked. She hurried down the ladder, coming over and putting a hand on Cassidy's shoulder. Harris stood on her other side, the painting forgotten.

"Is it that bad?" Harris asked apprehensively.

"I was driving."

Weighty silence descended. Cassidy's body flushed hot then cold.

"Oh, my goodness." Kelly put her hand over her mouth. Then wrapped both arms around Cassidy.

"No." Harris gasped. She hurried over and joined the hug.

"Yes." Pain sliced through her inside at what Torque had suffered. For her.

After a while, Kelly pulled back. "He went to prison for you?"

"He told me to leave and never breathe a word."

"This explains why you refuse to touch your trust fund. You couldn't stand living it up when he was locked up." Understanding dawned over Harris's face.

"Right."

Kelly crossed her arms. "And why you insisted on not only becoming an attorney but taking the county defender's position. Why you've spent so much time and money on Miss Betty—the widow. Why you've done so much with me on my charity projects. Maybe even why you've adopted and why you're adopting again."

"Yes, yes, and yes." A weight had been lifted from her chest, just by telling someone, and she felt pounds lighter.

Harris tapped her chin. "And it's why you pushed for the mentor program. It's why you asked for him."

Cassidy hung her head. "Yes."

Kelly shook her head. "You've been punishing yourself."

"I couldn't stand the guilt."

"Wait. Did you ask him to do it?" Harris asked.

"No."

Kelly's jaw dropped. "Why did he?"

"I don't know. He would never say. And to top it all off, I wasn't supposed to be driving. He never let me. I just jumped into his truck and took off. He happened to see me and was able to get in the passenger side. He buckled my seatbelt, or I might have been killed, too."

"Was his buckled?" Harris asked.

"No. That's why he broke his leg."

Kelly shook her head and gave Cassidy another quick hug. "I can't believe you didn't get hurt at all."

"I didn't. I wondered about that over the years, too. But his truck was an old 1970s model. Heavy. Built like a tank. We weren't going that fast, but it was fast enough. I was bruised some, and really shook up, but not hurt."

"And you left," Harris stated flatly.

"Yes."

"Because he told you to."

"Yes."

Chapter 15

Torque shut the lights off in the garage. Another satisfying day filled with honest labor. Would he ever tire of the privilege of working?

He should have gone home. Gram was old and hadn't made the trip out to Pittsburgh to see him much. He vowed when he got out that he'd spend as much time with her as he could, but his feet had a mind of their own, apparently, and he turned the corner to Cassidy's apartment complex just before eight twenty.

A young man and woman stood under the pole light. The woman wore tight black pants, a long-sleeved t-shirt, and sneakers. Her hair was in a ponytail. The sweet scent of weed drifted over the fall air. Cassidy couldn't take her kids out of this place fast enough. He intended to tell her that again as soon as he got up there.

He cursed the two dollars in his pocket. He'd have brought her supper if he had more than two dollars to his name.

Passing the couple, he nodded. They didn't even try to hide their joint. The woman's glassy eyes looked him over, and with boldness supplied by the grass, she smiled. "Nice shoulders."

"Shut up," the man said. "Hand it over." He held his hand out for the joint.

Torque kept walking, hoping his irritation with Cassidy's living arrangements subsided enough for him to have an intelligent conversation instead of the litany of demands that wanted to pop out of his mouth.

Taking the stairs two at a time, he reached her floor. He rapped on her door. Even though it was closed, he could hear one, or both, of the twins screaming. He rapped again, louder.

His hand was raised to rap a third time when the door opened. Jamal held a screaming Nessa. Nissa clung to his leg, crying just as loud.

Torque walked in, scooping Nissa off the floor and closing and locking the door behind him. "Where's your mother?" he asked in a near-shout to be heard over the noise. His eyes scanned the apartment. It looked like it'd been ransacked. Fear tightened his throat. His stomach twisted.

"She went out."

"What?" His eyes snapped back to Jamal.

"She went out."

She went out. "On a date?"

Jamal nodded.

Torque swallowed, surprised at the pain in his chest. It's what he wanted. It's what he told her to do. Crap.

"Who's watching you?" He looked around again. Was the babysitter in the bathroom?

"She left."

It was too hard to try to have a conversation over the crying babies. "Have you eaten?"

Jamal shook his head. He pointed to an unopened package of spaghetti and a can of sauce on the counter.

Good grief, that would take thirty minutes to make—the water had to be heated and the noodles boiled. He couldn't listen to the crying for that long.

Rooting through the cupboards, he found soup crackers. He ripped the package open and dug out two crackers. Both of the babies quit crying to gum the crackers.

He found sippy cups and soon had both of the girls in their high chairs with a pile of crackers in front of them. Quiet.

Now that it was quiet enough that he could talk to Jamal, he asked, "You want to help me make eggs?" He opened the fridge and pulled out a carton.

"Sure."

"Let's get a bowl, and you can crack 'em. One each for the girls, and I bet you eat two."

Jamal grinned. "Bet I do, too."

He found some frozen broccoli and a bit of cheese.

He had just dished out the makeshift omelets and started to feed the twins when there was a pounding on the door. "Let me in, kid."

Jamal's eyes got big. "It's her. She told me not to leave the living room."

"What?"

"She told me to stay in the living room with the twins. She said my sisters weren't to leave it and neither was I. If I did, she said she was going to take a wooden spoon and smack us all." His lower lip trembled. "I had to leave to let you in."

Torque put a hand on Jamal's arm as he stood. "You're fine. She's not coming back in here, and she won't touch you or your sisters. Not with a spoon. Not with anything else."

He met Jamal's eyes with a serious look of his own. "Keep an eye on your sisters, bud. I'll be right back." He stood and strode to the door as the pounding continued.

He yanked the door open, and the woman who had been outside smoking a joint almost fell into him.

Her eyes widened as she recognized him. She recovered quickly. "Who said you were allowed to be in here? You better not have harmed those innocent little children. Get out." She tried to push past.

He didn't move, and she was forced to stop.

Gripping the door like it was her throat, he said real low and real slow, "Get out. Don't come back."

Her eyes narrowed. She huffed. He didn't flinch.

Her nostrils flared. "I will be calling the police on you."

"Do it from the hall." He pushed the door shut. She stumbled out, caught her balance, and turned, but it was too late. He had the door closed and locked. She started pounding on it and yelling.

Torque turned. Jamal watched him with wide eyes. He'd not considered that the boy might be taking it all in. He smiled, hoping it looked natural and not like he was gritting his teeth.

Jamal returned his smile, a bit shaky.

He couldn't believe that the woman, who had just been standing outside smoking a joint, would actually call the police. If he never had a run-in with the cops for the rest of his life, he would not be disappointed. But technically, she was supposed to be here, and he wasn't.

"You okay, bud?" He touched Jamal's shoulder. He flinched. Torque moved his hand back. The little boy hadn't touched his food since Torque stood.

He nodded.

"You're going to have a story to tell your mom."

His lips curved up a little.

"Lost your appetite?"

He nodded. "It's like my old house. That mom was always mad."

Torque took a deep breath and blew it out. "I'm sorry. It made me angry that woman wasn't doing her job. She was supposed to be in here watching and playing with you."

"That's okay. It wasn't you. I'm glad you didn't let her back in." He shuddered.

The girls still had hearty appetites. Torque fed them, biting his tongue to keep from grilling Jamal about what, or rather who, Cassidy was with.

He tried to tell himself he hoped she found a man, a good man, since she deserved one, but Tough's words rang in his ears. "No man for her but you." That's how he felt. Tough's amazing ability to see what other people were thinking and feeling was kind of legendary in their family, but he couldn't have nailed his thoughts any better.

Unless they were Tough's thoughts?

Torque had never stopped to think that Tough hadn't read his mind. Did Tough really feel that he was the only man for Cassidy?

"Want some ketchup for those?" he asked Jamal.

The boy nodded.

Torque went to the fridge and got the bottle. If he were eating eggs, he'd have them slathered in ketchup. Maybe that would bring back Jamal's appetite. He wasn't sure why he was so concerned about food. First Cassidy eating, now Jamal. They were poor when he was growing up, but they were never hungry. There had always been mac and cheese.

The ketchup helped, and Jamal ended up finishing his eggs by the time Torque had the girls' trays cleared off and wiped. He pursed his lips, looking at their sloppy, smiling faces. He'd washed plenty of trucks in his time, but he'd never washed a little girl's face before. Now he had two.

"Little help here, Jamal?" He lifted a brow.

Jamal snickered. Torque's own lips curved up. He probably made quite a picture. His hands and forearms were clean, but his t-shirt was covered in dirt and grease. His face probably was too. Because of the chaos when he stepped in, he'd never taken his ball cap off, and it was filthy. He had to admit, it felt good to have the dirt of honest labor on him. But it probably did look funny to see the dirty, tough ex-con standing in front of the high chairs, overwhelmed by two tiny little girls.

They babbled to each other. They each had just two shiny white front teeth, and they flashed occasionally as they banged their trays and laughed at each other.

Jamal finally decided to be helpful. "They like the cloth to be warm."

He lifted a brow at Jamal in mock consternation. "Thanks."

It couldn't be that hard. After rinsing the cloth with warm water, he sized up the nearest twin and tried to get the dried egg off her face.

She had more experience than he did and easily ducked away from his hand.

"They hate having their faces wiped."

"I see."

"Mom just does it. Fast so they can't get away."

"Hmm." That might be helpful. But there were a lot of cracks and creases. It wasn't like a windshield. More like an aluminum rim with fancy studs. Only he'd never tried to wash a wheel while it was moving.

If he could survive ten years in prison, he surely ought to be able to wash a baby's face.

"You can do it," Jamal said earnestly.

He hadn't even had a cheerleader in prison. *You could have. Cassidy would have supported you. She tried. And you shut her down.*

She'd eventually quit. Except on holidays. She'd never given up on Christmas.

Focus, man.

It took him two tries, but he was able to swoop down and gently grab Nessa's face before she averted it. He hadn't realized how hard dried egg was to wipe off.

Eventually he had two little girls with shiny clean faces and somewhat clean hands. Just in time, too, since Nissa had wiggled herself half out of the high chair.

"She's like Houdini."

"What's that?" Jamal asked as he took his plate to the sink.

"It was a man who could get out of some pretty tight spots."

Figuring out how to open the high chair was not hard. Figuring out how to pick up the wiggling baby and fighting the sudden anxiety that he might drop her was much harder.

Jamal was equal parts helpful advisor and laughing spectator. Torque couldn't blame him. If he'd been watching one of his brothers do what he was doing, he'd be laughing his butt off.

Finally, both girls were on the ground, the high chairs wiped and slid to their places along the wall, and the supper mess cleaned up.

Holy smokes. He felt like he did as much work since he'd stepped into this apartment as he'd done all day at the garage. He glanced at the wall clock. Wow. Nine thirty. Where did the time go?

"What time was your mom going to be home?" Torque asked Jamal as they settled down on the living room floor.

"She told the woman eleven."

"I see. So, you have school tomorrow?"

"Yep."

"Homework?"

"Mom made me do it before she left."

"What time is bedtime?"

Jamal smiled slyly. "The girls go to bed at eight."

Torque snorted. "Okay. They're a little late tonight."

"Yep. And you need to change their diapers and put sleepers on them." He crossed his arms over his narrow chest. "I'm watching, because this is gonna be good."

"You could do it for me."

"When I want my mom to do my homework for me, she says I'll never learn it if someone else does it for me."

"Fabulous."

Torque eyed the babies. There were only two of them, but it seemed like they were always going in a hundred different directions. He could get elbow deep in nuts, bolts, pistons, and rods, get them working in perfect time, and put five hundred horses on the ground with all the confidence of a grizzly in a flock of sheep.

But he was downright intimidated by the innocent eyes and chubby limbs of Jamal's sisters.

He pushed off the floor. "At least they're not crying."

"Yet," Jamal said, getting up. Apparently to get into a better position to watch the show.

"Thanks for the encouragement." He stood with his hands on his hips. People did this all the time. Cassidy did this every day. He could figure it out.

In the end, it was just as hard as he thought it was going to be. Chasing one twin while trying to wrestle the clothes off the other. He finally put one in her crib and focused his attention on the other. Jamal handed him the clean diaper and sleeper, neither of which came with an owner's manual or any other kind of instruction.

"How hard would it be to ink directions on every diaper?" he asked under his breath.

"You could write to the manufacturer."

"Really?" That seemed like a mature statement for a little boy.

"Mom says if you don't like something, don't sit around and complain about it. Do something."

"I see. I like your mom."

Jamal nodded. "Me too."

"Does she go out a lot?"

"Usually she takes us with her."

"Oh."

"But we went to the park for a little bit after school before I had to come home and do homework. Mom had to get ready to go."

Torque swallowed against the tightness in his throat and wished he hadn't brought the subject up. The chubby leg in his hand kicked and twisted, not wanting to get shoved into the leg of the sleeper. He finally had it in and the snaps done up before he realized he'd not lined the snaps up correctly and had to take them all out. She managed to wiggle a foot out, and he basically had to stuff the whole baby back into her clothes. This time, he double-checked that he had the snaps lined up.

He did better with the second baby, but it still took a good half hour to get them changed and dressed, and Jamal had been right. They were both crying by the time he was done.

Holding the twins, one on each hip, while Jamal got his teeth brushed, Torque apologized that he wasn't going to be able to read like he'd seen Cassidy do. Not with a crying twin in each hand. When she'd put them to bed, they'd just lain down and went to sleep.

"When they're up past their bedtime, they get fussy and cry easier."

Good to know. Now. Not that he could have done anything about it.

He tucked Jamal in the best he could with a crying baby in each arm and walked out to the living room, flipping the lights off with his elbow, until there was only a low glow from the light under the stove.

Ten thirty. He didn't want to put the babies down for the night while they were crying. Especially since he was a stranger to them and his would be the last face they saw. Kinda scary, even for an adult. So, he'd just suck it up and pace the floor with them.

Chapter 16

Cassidy had tried to call Elizabeth three times to let her know that she was going to be late, but the call kept going to a voice mail that wasn't set up.

Harris and Kelly had been so sweet and supportive after her guilty breakdown, but time had slipped away from her. Now, with Elizabeth not answering, Cassidy sped across town, attracting the attention of a town cop, who pulled out, lights flashing.

Cassidy slapped the steering wheel. She'd never gotten a traffic violation in her life before. After what happened that night with Torque, she was the world's biggest grandma driver.

But she needed to get home to her babies. Why wasn't Elizabeth answering? Could her phone be dead?

While the cop ran her license and insurance, she tried again. Still no answer.

"You're the model on the billboards." The cop, a young man, maybe mid-twenties, stuck his head in the car window.

"Yes, sir." Hopefully he'd let her go. She didn't even care about the fine.

"Have you been drinking?"

"Huh?" Seriously? Was he going to take all night?

He must not have liked the look on her face.

"I'd like you to get out of your car, miss. Slowly, keeping your hands in sight at all times."

She didn't roll her eyes and kept her features schooled in her courtroom mask as she got out of the car.

It took another twenty minutes, but they finally let her go with just a speeding fine. Normally she wouldn't have been too upset. They seemed like nice guys who were curious about the local celebrity whose picture was on the billboards. Or maybe they just wanted to see what she looked like in person. She got the curiosity, and it wasn't like she was so popular that it happened a lot. Still, the urge to get home to her children was a driving need that kept her barely civil.

She jerked to a stop in the parking lot and, grabbing her purse, raced into the apartment building and flew up the stairs, digging in her purse for her key. She slipped it in and opened the door carefully.

Dim, almost dark. Quiet. Hopefully that meant the kids were asleep.

She closed and locked the door, sniffing.

Torque. She identified his scent, strong, like he was here. Only he wasn't. Come to think of it, she hadn't seen Elizabeth's car in the lot. Not that she'd spent that much time looking, but it wasn't in the space where it was when Cassidy had left earlier.

The foreboding that something wasn't right washed over her hard and fast, like a rogue wave. She swallowed, setting her purse on the counter and softly walking farther in.

There was a dark form on the couch. She walked closer as her eyes adjusted.

"Torque?" she whispered.

His eyes flew open. Wide and alarmed. His body didn't move, but every muscle seemed to tense, as though in preparation for an attack.

Cassidy froze for a second, not expecting her whispered word to have such a forceful impact.

His head twisted.

She realized he held a twin in each arm. Should she grab her babies? She didn't want him to think she was attacking him before he was fully awake.

"It's Cassidy."

He blinked. The board-like stiffness drained out of his body.

She relaxed.

"Hey," he said, his tone rough with sleep.

Her babies were safe. It eased the ball of anxiety in her chest. But Torque, looking sexy with sleep, ignited a whole new bundle of reactions.

"Is Jamal in bed?"

"Yeah."

"Where's Elizabeth?"

"Long story."

Uh. "Okay?" She reached down and gently lifted Nessa out of his left arm.

"They're changed and diapered, I just couldn't figure out how to set them down without waking them up."

Nessa shifted and let out a little squeak before snuggling down into Cassidy's shoulder.

Torque started to get up.

"You stay here. I can come back for Nessa."

"I can do it with one. I think."

She smiled and led the way back the hall. The door to Jamal's room was cracked, and she could see him sleeping soundly on his side.

The nightlight in the twins' room flickered as Torque followed her in. He watched as she kissed Nessa's forehead and laid her gently in the crib. Holding Nissa, he waited for her to kiss her forehead then imitated her movements, his large hands cradling the little girl, as he set her gently down. Cassidy covered her with her blanket, and they tiptoed out.

Torque spoke as soon as they got to the kitchen. "I'm sorry. I'm filthy. I probably got grease on their sleeper things and maybe on your couch. It was kind of crazy, and I never took my boots off..."

"Shh." She placed a finger over his lips which stopped his words faster than a plug in a drain.

His body did the whole stiffening thing again, but this time, it seemed to be from her touch, which gave her a feeling of power, not unpleasant.

"What are you doing here?" Her finger dropped.

"Your babysitter was smoking pot in the parking lot. She left Jamal up here to watch the twins. Told him if he left the living room she was smacking everyone with a spoon." He shoved a hand in his pocket. "I didn't actually hear her say that. It came from Jamal."

Cassidy ground her teeth together. She would definitely be taking steps to deal with Elizabeth tomorrow, although she guessed the woman would be gone. People might not believe a nine-year-old, but Torque's testimony would stand. The nanny agency would be hearing from her too.

"Were they okay?" She had just seen them, handled them, but her heart ached. Her babies in the hands of such a miserable person.

"Jamal had it under control. I think it hit him the hardest emotionally. Brought back some bad memories."

"He went to bed okay?"

"I haven't heard him." His jaw ticked. "I didn't hear you come in either."

She smiled. "I know."

His mouth opened like he was going to ask her something, but then he looked over her head, closing it.

"I appreciate you coming in. You could have called. I have a landline."

He shrugged, his wide shoulders distracting her. "I didn't know."

"The phone is in my bedroom."

"I wasn't in there." Somehow the gravelly tone of his voice sent shivers up and down her spine.

He shifted, and she searched her mind for something to say to keep him from leaving.

"I guess the nanny idea isn't working out so well."

"Prisons aren't the only place full of nasty people."

Which reminded her, she needed to tell him. "I told Harris and Kelly about what happened and why you went to prison."

He stopped looking over her head and met her eyes. "You shouldn't have." He searched her face. "Tonight? You told them tonight?"

"Yes. Up until tonight, no one knew."

He shook his head. "No one needs to know." He paused. "I thought you were on a date."

"Is that what Elizabeth said?"

"Elizabeth pounded on the door, demanded to be allowed in, and insisted she was going to call the cops on me. We didn't really have a rational conversation."

"I see."

"Yeah. Jamal said you went out. I guess I assumed the date part."

"I went to the new children's activity center that Kelly is opening next week to help her paint. Harris Winsted, our friend and the librarian, was there too."

His eyes flicked down over her outfit. Surely the bright paint she was using was visible. It was on her face and arms. Her t-shirt was splattered with it. And it was probably in her hair too, which was shoved up in a sloppy bun that probably looked like yesterday's leftovers.

"You never look at me."

"Too tempting," he murmured. Then he stirred, breaking eye contact and moving to go. She wasn't going to stop him. It was late, he was tired, and she wasn't chasing him. No matter what her friends said about why he did what he did.

He thought she was tempting?

Her mouth opened. "You never said why you were here to begin with."

He shrugged a big shoulder. "Stopped in after work to check on you."

"Check on me? Like make sure I'm doing all those things you told me to do?"

"I'm sorry." He adjusted his ball cap, his muscles bulging, like he was fighting with himself. He turned back to her, closing the gap between them.

"I do see you." He took her shoulders. "You're beautiful, smart, compassionate... All those things that you were in high school have matured into a woman who's done so much good and has so much potential for more." His eyes dipped down, and his breath became unsteady. "You're beautiful, Cassidy. But the whole world already knows that. Don't think for one second that I don't know it too." His voice lowered. "I know it."

He brought his thumb up and traced her lip. She shivered.

"I could spend all day just looking at you, watching you, the way you move, the crease you get between your eyes when you're thinking. I love your toes and the sharp angles of your ankles. I love the intelligence that sits deep in your eyes when you look at me. I love the way I feel when you stand beside me..." He trailed off, and his eyes unfocused. "I feel like a motor that has the final piece in place and is running in perfect tune. That's how it is when I'm with you. Like you're the other piece of me, and I'm running in time."

His eyes dropped, and his hand came up to cup her cheek. "I see you, Cassie."

Her heart thrilled at the nickname he'd used in high school. Once. No one else ever called her that. Her hands came up and slid around the hard sides of his stomach. His body trembled. Her whole arms tingled.

"You're everything I want. I have to remind myself I can't have you. Not looking makes it easier."

Her heart beat like a judge's gavel trying to restore order in an out-of-control courtroom. His face was only millimeters from hers. The same small space separated their bodies. She pressed closer, and they were touching.

He groaned. Low. Anguished. His face dropped, and his lips replaced his thumb, light and soft.

She closed her eyes. Her hands slid up the hard ridges of his back.

He let out another guttural sound, and his arms came around her, crushing her to him. The soft tingle of his lips on hers was replaced by a blazing heat as their mouths fused. The burning emotion that had lay banked in her body for years came roaring back to life, and suddenly she couldn't get enough. Colors exploded behind her closed eyes. The world spun and heated and tilted crazily, while the only solid thing was Torque under her hands, his mouth on hers, his hands around her, pressing her against him.

The kiss lasted an eternity and yet was too short. He pulled away, his breathing erratic. His hands ran up and down her back, feeling the tilt of her shoulders and the curve of her waist.

"I'll not wonder what I'm missing anymore. I'll know. And it will make it a million times worse for me." He dropped little, loving kisses up her face to her forehead, before tucking her head under his chin. "I'm sorry. Not for kissing you. For making it worse." His chest jerked under her cheek as he snorted a laugh. "Maybe that didn't shatter your world like it did mine."

Her arms tightened, and her eyes closed. It didn't matter that he'd come from work and was covered in dirt. In his arms, she was home.

She cleared her throat, hoping she didn't sound like she'd swallowed a whistle when she spoke. "I've dreamed about that for a long time. It was definitely better than I'd imagined it to be."

"It'd get better with practice." There was a smile in his voice.

She smiled against his chest then lifted her head. "I'm willing to practice."

His teeth flashed white in the darkness. He palmed her head and tucked it back under his chin. "Me too. More than willing." His fingers worked in the back of her head. With a small tug, her hair came free.

Immediately his hands were in it. His heart stuttered against her cheek. "You smell good. Feel good. Look good."

He could run his hands through her hair all night long.

"But I'm not doing you any favors right now."

"Maybe it would work out with the adoption agency."

His chest moved under her cheek. A deep, silent sigh. "Men don't go to prison because they're boy scouts."

"You didn't do anything."

"Stop saying that. I paid the price. This is part of it. You wouldn't have adopted Jamal if you'd paid. You wouldn't be fostering the babies."

He was right. She knew it. She probably knew it just as well as he, since she was a public defender. It was just that when one wanted something as badly as she did, rational thought had a tendency to disappear.

"Thank you." She wished there was more she could say or do.

"I've figured out a way to keep those lips occupied, so you'd better stop saying that."

She smiled. "For a smart man, you're awfully slow sometimes."

He grinned back. "I was too busy looking at you to think about what to do with you."

"Wish I could have seen you change those diapers tonight."

His ears turned red. "Get Jamal to tell you about it in the morning. Poor kid's stomach muscles will be sore from all the laughing he did."

"I bet." She could only hope Jamal took a video.

"That and trying to get them stuffed into their sleepers."

She nodded. "It's not easy."

His fingers trailed over her back. "I'm spending the week at Mrs. Ford's garage. Know where it is?"

"I think so." She'd never been there, but she knew where the hill was that Mrs. Ford's house sat on. She made a mental note to call the contacts that she'd made today back and let them know where they could send the work.

"Jamal's welcome to spend some time there after school if you want to drop him off. Can't really watch the twins for you unless you have a cage to put them in."

"They make play yards." She didn't really need him to watch the twins, but it could be an excuse for her to see him.

"Bring 'em."

"Just for this week?"

"Definitely this week. I don't know about next."

"Okay. Did someone open Tyke's old garage?"

"Me."

Her head popped up. "Torque, that's wonderful!"

"Yeah. Just everything has to work out."

"I'm sure it will."

He wasn't as sure, but he had a lot of hope.

"Listen." He leaned back far enough to cup her cheeks in his hands. "I don't want you to think I haven't dreamed about us or that what I feel for you isn't strong and beating on the inside of my chest like pistons in an engine." His hands shook. "But those kids need you. And I'm in the way."

"*I* need you."

He shook his head. "Look at what you've done without me."

"I want you."

"I want you." He lifted his hands from her face and held them up. "So much I'm trembling with it." He backed up, and she let her hands slide away.

"There's got to be a way." The words came out in a passionate whisper.

"When you find it, you let me know." He gave a little smile. "We're friends?"

Her throat clogged, and her voice sounded broken. "I know that's what it has to be."

"Good. You come to grips with that, and I'll try not to rip the throat out of whatever man you find to be a daddy to those little ones." His smile looked more like a snarl with teeth.

She wanted to say she'd find a way around. That there was a possibility for them. But it wasn't true. And she wasn't sure how far she'd actually go to keep the twins that she considered hers. Would she marry a stranger? What if that ended up like the nanny situation? She supposed she could divorce him, but there would be custody issues...unless she had an ironclad prenup. It would work. But that would mean walking away from Torque. She couldn't forget that he'd not walked away from her. He'd stood among the wreckage and taken the hit.

He was right. But she walked over to where he'd stopped by the counter and slipped her hands around his waist again. "Kiss me goodbye. Make it a long one." She'd never tried to be seductive, but it came out low and husky and it worked on Torque like a torch to gas. And she went up right along with him.

Chapter 17

"How would you feel about going to the garage with me today," Torque asked his gram when he walked into the kitchen before daylight the next morning.

She sat at the kitchen table, her Bible open in front of her. Same place she'd been every morning of his life.

Her old blue eyes lifted in surprise. "Really? You can do that?"

"Sure. Probably. Mrs. Ford was there most of the day yesterday with her quilting or something. I remember you being a part of that years ago." He'd missed so much time with his gram, and he'd figured last night—the small amount of time that he'd not spent reliving every second of his kisses with Cassidy—that he could spend time with Gram and she'd enjoy renewing her quilting friends.

Gram nodded slowly. "Can't believe you remember."

"How could I forget? They gave us boys all a quilt after Mom died." A little pang always touched his heart when he thought about her dying. It didn't hurt as bad as it used to. He supposed there'd always be a hole in his heart where she used to be.

"Yes. Kind of them." She rose slowly and reached for her cane. "I need to get ready and pack a bag. I assumed we won't be coming home until late."

"You can drive us over and leave whenever you want. I've been walking."

"I know, son. I thought your license renewal came in the mail?"

It had. He just didn't have the money to get it. Actually, he had that check from John in the drawer. But he supposed his checking account at the bank had been closed due to inactivity, and he'd need to open another one.

"Does Shelly still work at the bank?" he asked Gram as she puttered around the kitchen, getting ready.

"Lands, no. She quit years ago after her second baby was born."

Well, he didn't remember anyone else. Better put that on his to-do list. Right under "Forget about Cassidy" and "Don't think about Cassidy" and "Definitely don't think about kissing Cassidy." There were other things on his list, but those were the ones running through his mind.

"I'm ready whenever you are." He opened the door to the fridge. His eyes landed on the eggs. Was Cassidy up cooking breakfast for the kids? It'd be more fun with two people in the kitchen. Heck, yeah, he could think of a lot of ways to have fun in the kitchen with Cassidy.

He stared at the fridge. What was he even going to get? He couldn't remember and shut the door.

He was able to get Gram settled in the same spot Mrs. Ford had been the day before. Dragging the office chair out and placing it companionably beside his gram, he made sure she was fine then went back to the office and started the computer. He'd been dreading this part. He hadn't worked with computers much before he went to prison, and now that he was out, everything seemed to be computerized.

It was disconcerting to say the least. They had some old dinosaurs in the prison for the inmates to work on, and he'd put some time in there, just because he'd figured it was necessary. Thankfully the computer on the desk was about the same age as the ones in the prison, and he was actually able to get it on.

Yesterday Tom had asked him to email his estimate to the insurance company. He hadn't sent an email in years and wasn't sure how to start. Out of desperation more than inspiration, he finally typed in "how do I send an email" and started to get things figured out.

It felt like he was finally making some progress, although he still needed to type up the estimate from his handwritten notes, when a customer pulled in. Turned out to be someone Turbo had sent. He got right to work replacing the brakes and drums, waved at Mrs. Ford when he realized she was sitting with Gram in the chair he'd gotten for her, and promptly lost track of all time. Inmates had talked about getting in the "zone," but none of them ever described it about their work. Kissing Cassidy had taken over the number one spot on his list of things he loved to do, as he'd figured it would, which is why he'd resisted for so long. But doing diesel repair was a close second.

Gram and Miss Angelina made him stop for fifteen minutes and eat lunch. Another two customers came in, bringing enough work for two more days, and Tough stopped by. After looking things over, he made a parts run, coming back with his old Ford—one or two models newer than a Model T, at least that's how Torque described it—loaded down with boxes and hoses and clamps, nuts, bolts, and other odds and ends. Tough unloaded it all at the front of the garage. Torque didn't realize what he'd been doing until he stepped around the back of the truck he was changing the airbag on.

"What's this?" He put his hands on his hips.

Tough dropped a box, which sounded heavy, and strode casually back out to his truck.

'Course he wasn't going to answer. It was Tough after all. Torque figured if you couldn't beat 'em, join 'em, and he helped finish unloading the old pickup.

Tough disappeared into the office for a few minutes, while Torque looked through the stuff on the floor. Several thousand dollars' worth of truck parts.

Tough came to the door of the office and stuck a hand against the jamb, leaning on it. "I left the receipts in the desk drawer. They're paid. I'll come looking for reimbursement after Christmas." He slapped the jamb and walked forward. "I left a thousand bucks in cash beside those receipts. That's yours."

"I'm not taking a grand from you."

"Figured you wouldn't. 'Member that dent in the bumper of your pulling truck, you couldn't figure out what happened?"

Torque nodded slowly, vaguely remembering the big Texas bumper he'd had on his pulling truck. So big and low, it'd almost dragged on the ground. He'd spent hours putting hundreds of dollars' worth of lights in it. Someone had taken it for a joyride and dented the bumper beyond repair. Since he'd been the one who left the keys in the truck, he was the one who had paid the garage he worked for, and who owned the truck, for the repairs.

He'd never figured out who did it.

"Me." Tough gave a little grin. "Gotta get back to the shop."

Torque shoved his shoulder, turning him so he could grab his hand. Tough allowed it, grabbing Torque's hand and putting his other arm around his back, pulling him in for a brotherly hug. Torque fought the sting of tears. His brothers had come through for him in a way he hadn't imagined.

Tough pulled back and started out the door. "Talk to Turbo. He charmed that lady at the bank years ago to do something special with your account. You'll have to sign something to get it reopened, but all the money's there, minus a few fees, probably."

"I'll do it. Thanks."

Tough left, and Torque went back to work, back in his happy place where a man earned his bread with his hands and the labor of a strong back.

Jamal's voice broke into his concentration, and he couldn't believe three hours had flown by. He grinned from the creeper when the little boy's head popped under the truck. "I found him."

His grin faded as Cassidy's feet came into view. How could a woman be so perfect that even her feet made his heart pound?

He slid out and rolled to his feet. "Hey."

Her smile warmed his heart. "I left the twins in the car so they would stay clean. I can't stay."

"That's fine. I'll bring Jamal home, probably around eight." He wished he weren't so dirty, because his hands itched to slide around her waist and ease the knots out of her back, but it was probably better if he didn't touch her.

"Are you sure you don't mind?" Cassidy bit her lip.

He looked at Jamal who stood to the side, listening. He grinned at the boy. Maybe Jamal wouldn't end up being a mechanic, but Torque could remember his own childhood and how he'd loved hanging out at the garage. It had given him a sense of purpose and direction and had made him feel like he belonged somewhere.

"Jamal is welcome to be here anytime."

She smiled again, and Torque's heart quivered. "Oh." She dug into her purse. "I got you this." She pulled out a phone. "I got it during my lunch hour. I actually *took* a lunch hour. There's a plan with it. If I stuck it on with mine, I got a deal, so I did that to begin with. We'll work things out later. Anyway, if you need some help figuring things out, Jamal helped me figure out mine, so he's gold with that."

Torque gritted his teeth. It galled to take something from her. He wanted to be the provider. But at the same time, his whole body felt gratitude that she'd thought of him and taken the time to do something this considerate.

"Don't even look at me like that. You're taking this. And this," she held up a sticky note, "has your new number and the passcode I had to put on your phone. It's all set up and ready to use."

His mouth opened then closed.

"Just say 'thanks,'" she said, one hand on her hip.

"Thanks."

"I'm taking it in and setting it on your desk."

"Okay."

The ladies had been quietly sitting in the corner, and Torque had kind of forgotten about them. "Come back out, and I'll introduce you to the Kicking Quilters."

Her brow furrowed, but her lips tilted up. "Okay?"

"Come on, Jamal."

Jamal skipped after him. He introduced his gram and Miss Angelina. By the time they'd asked him how old he was and what grade he was in, Cassidy was back.

"And this is his mother, Cassidy Kimball."

His gram's eyes narrowed, as though she was remembering something. He didn't think she knew about him meeting Cassidy, and she definitely didn't know about the accident, or at least shouldn't. But Gram had ways of finding things out. When he was really young, he felt like she had spies out everywhere.

"Good to meet you, Cassidy," Miss Angelina said.

They shook hands and chatted a bit.

"I need to run. The girls are in the car." She waved a paper in the air. "I assume you had this estimate in there by the computer because you needed to type it out and send it?"

"Yeah." Torque rubbed his neck. "I just haven't gotten to it." He'd rather be out fixing something than sitting in front of the computer, frustrated.

"I think I can get that done at home before you get there."

"You don't have to."

"I have a few briefs I need to go over, and a couple of other things, but maybe if you stay and help Jamal with his homework?"

"It's a deal."

Jamal smiled and held his fist out. Torque bumped it. Cassidy gave them a look he didn't quite get then waved the paper and walked away.

Miss Angelina said, "Let me know next time if Jamal is going to be here after school. Little boys come home hungry and need a snack." She set her quilting down and looked at Gram. "Want to come with me? I think I can still find something that would help a little stomach feel happy."

Gram nodded, and they stood up together.

Jamal's mouth opened like he couldn't quite believe that someone so old could know so much about little boys.

Torque turned back to the truck he'd been working on. "You ever been in a garage, Jamal?"

"Nope."

"Well, this is called a creeper. There's another one leaning against the wall over there. See it?"

"Yep."

"Grab that, and you can roll under here with me. I'm just tightening the nuts up on this airbag. I'll teach you what a wrench is."

"Rad." Jamal skipped over and grabbed the creeper, doing exactly what Torque would have done at his age, which was to set it on the floor and use it like a skateboard to come back to the truck.

Time flew by, and it was seven thirty before he knew it. Jamal had mentioned that he was hungry a few times, and Torque's own stomach was rumbling.

They cleaned the garage, took Miss Angelina up to her house, and drove Gram home where Torque took a five-minute shower and changed out of his dirty clothes before Jamal and he walked to the apartment. Torque had his phone and handed it to Jamal.

"I've been teaching you some garage stuff. How about you see if you can crack my thick head about this?"

"Piece of cake." Jamal took the phone and started swiping and clicking.

"Whoa. Slow down. Like way down."

"Old man."

"Ouch."

"Truth hurts."

"Sure does. Start out with something simple. Like, how do I make calls on it?"

Jamal went slower, and by the time they'd reached the apartment, Torque was pretty confident he could at least make his own phone calls.

Cassidy opened the door after their first knock. Immediately Torque could tell something serious was wrong. Her eyes were pinched and red, her mouth tight, her smile forced. She hadn't changed from her work clothes and still wore her heels.

Supper was on the table, however, and the twins were happy in their high chairs. Jamal didn't notice anything amiss, and Cassidy shook her head at Torque's questioning look. He didn't have the right to reach out and put his arm around her as he longed to do, but it only took him three-quarters of a second to do it anyway.

She sagged against him immediately. He wrapped both arms around her. He tilted his head down and whispered in her ear. "You're telling me after the kids are in bed, right?"

"Yes." Her voice cracked, and Torque's heart broke. Whatever had her so upset, he wanted to fix it right now. He fisted his hands behind her back, trying to resist the urge to do something.

They sat at the table, and he helped her feed the twins. Jamal put away two platefuls in between rambling almost nonstop about all the exciting things he'd done at the garage. It made Cassidy smile, which eased some of the tightness in Torque's chest.

Jamal took a shower while Torque cleaned up the table and Cassidy got the twins down and ready for their bath. Torque helped Jamal with his homework, then Cassidy read to him. All in all, the evening flew by, but Torque could barely contain himself by the time Cassidy walked slowly out from the hall.

He wasn't used to seeing her shoulders slumped and her head down. The Cassidy he knew was confident. A problem-solver. Smart and resourceful. Whatever happened had blown all that away.

Putting his arm around her, he led her to the couch where she sagged into the cushions. He sat on the floor at her feet, taking her heels off. She sighed.

Gently rubbing the feet he'd admired earlier in the day while she leaned her head on the back of the couch and closed her eyes, he waited.

Finally, without opening her eyes, she said, "I typed your estimate up. You can check it if you want, and then I can email it wherever it needs to go."

"Thanks."

"Did you have email...before?"

"Yeah."

"Maybe you can check if you still have it?"

"I'll do that." He used his thumbs to press small circles on the arch of her foot. "Thanks for the phone."

She opened one eye and looked at him. "You know it's the least of what I owe you."

"I won this discussion the last time we had it."

A shadow of a smile crossed her face. "I'm a lawyer, and we don't like losing arguments."

"Pick a different one, and I'll let you win."

Her mouth flattened, and she leaned her head back, closing her eyes again. "The adoption agency called today. They've just approved a couple who are interested in adopting the twins. They want them to visit a couple nights next week and spend next Saturday with them."

His hands stilled on her feet. No wonder she was so depressed.

"I told them I was getting a nanny, and that I'd contacted a real estate agent and was planning on buying a house in the next month, but it didn't matter."

Torque stroked the top of her bare foot. "It didn't matter because they'd already decided these people get to adopt or didn't matter because you hadn't found a father?"

"It was just the caseworker and not her boss, but I'd already been told if I had a husband, or was close to having a husband, it would be a green light, so..." She shrugged. Her chin trembled, but so quickly, he almost missed it.

How could this be so hard? With all his heart, he wanted to help Cassidy, but doing so would mean finding her a man that wasn't him and giving her up completely. Funny, he was finding it harder to do that than he'd found it to volunteer to go to prison for her.

He cleared his throat and started slowly. "Turbo just helped pave a driveway this week." He named a town thirty-five minutes away. He took a deep breath, sliding his hand around Cassidy's foot in a soft caress. "The man's a doctor, an orthopedic surgeon. He lost his wife and daughters two years ago in a car accident when they were out west visiting her parents. Turbo talked to him for a while." He stopped and looked up at her. "You don't know Turbo, but he's everyone's friend." She nodded, shaking her head at the same time, which made Torque's mouth kick up a little, despite the crushing pressure in his chest. "Somehow the guy told Turbo that he'd just started trying online dating in the last two months, and it'd been a bust for him." His hand skimmed over the soft warmth of her foot. He touched the veins, traced the long, slender toes, felt the longing that bored out of his chest and down his arms, making them heavy and achy, like hard work never could.

He forced his hands to still and for his face to turn up, meeting her gaze. "Turbo told him about you."

"So you started a 'find Cassidy a husband' campaign?" Her jaw stuck out.

Silence settled on the small apartment as they stared at each other. He shook his head. "I didn't 'just start' anything. I'm just continuing what I've always done, and that is I'll do whatever it takes to make you happy."

"You don't think I'd be happy choosing my own husband?"

"You'd rather have the twins. They need you. You love them like they're yours."

She opened her mouth to say something but closed it and swallowed her words.

"The man is ready to remarry. He's open to having children. And he'd be okay with adopting. Turbo actually called pretending to be a patient and talked to his receptionist, his nurse, and the surgical ward at the hospital where he works. He's well-liked and respected. Turbo's just waiting on permission to forward your number to him."

Cassidy leaned forward, taking his face in her hands. He lost his balance and fell backward, and she followed him off the couch and onto the floor, her hand cupping his cheeks, her body warm against his. He closed his eyes against the overwhelming need to press her closer.

"I already know who I want. He keeps trying to give me away."

He shook his head and looked over her shoulder. "You're going to have to choose."

The shadow in her eye and the flicker of her lip as it tightened showed that she knew he was right.

He twisted so they were lying on their sides facing each other. He brushed a hair off her soft cheek. "If there was any way in the world they'd consider an ex-con just out of prison, I'd be begging you to take me. But we both know it's not going to happen."

She bit her lip.

He'd lost track of the number of stories he'd heard from inmates who'd been in prison and released and back in about the stigma that followed a convict. He'd been lucky enough to get out and fall into the arms of his family. Of his brothers and Cassidy, really, but still. Not everyone had relatives who weren't criminals.

"So you have to choose." His hand slid into her hair, and his thumb traced her angled jaw. "I don't want you to hurt, and those babies need you, so I'm trying to make it as easy as possible for you." He gave a humorless laugh. "Except I can't stay away."

Her breath came fast and mingled with his. Her eyes lowered, their noses almost touching. "Let Turbo give him your number." Each word stabbed at his heart like a fork. "Please." The fork twisted. He didn't want another man to have her, couldn't stand the thought of another man touching this soft skin, threading his hands into her hair, breathing her breath, but it hurt almost as much to think about her losing her babies and Jamal losing his sisters.

It was a sacrifice he had no choice but to make.

Her eyes darkened, and he could feel the pain seeping from them, could almost taste her heartache. But she, too, had to be thinking of Jamal and his sisters, because her eyes hardened and her jaw clenched.

"Okay."

She pushed herself off the floor, and he followed. She didn't meet his eyes. "I know you're trying to stay away, but I have plans to meet with my realtor tomorrow and look at a couple houses. I was hoping you could watch Jamal."

His heart clenched at the hurt in her tone. He'd done that. But she knew, as he did, that it was for the best. "Wouldn't it be more helpful for me to keep the girls?"

"I didn't figure you could, in the garage."

"Bring their cages."

Her lips tipped. "They're not cages."

"Gram and Miss Angelina will be there, and they talked about inviting their old friends from the quilting club they used to have twenty years ago. And if that doesn't work out, I'll quit at five like a normal person."

"Okay. That will be great. I appreciate it. I know Kelly will watch Jamal, although he'll be upset to miss out, since he seemed to have a great time with you today." She brushed her skirt off and picked up her shoes. Talking to him but not looking at him. He could grab her shoulders and turn her toward him, but that would only make it worse. She was putting distance between them, and that's what needed to be done.

"Bring him too. He's a help."

"You want me to drop three kids off at the garage where you're trying to work?"

"If you don't think I can handle it, do what you want." Torque turned toward the door. He couldn't stay longer. She didn't mean to insult him, she was just hurting and maybe trying to come to grips with what he'd already figured out: if she had a prayer of keeping her kids, she had to do it with someone else.

Right now, he could help by babysitting, but even that would have to end.

Chapter 18

Cassidy closed the door behind Torque and leaned against it. He was right. She knew it. But she didn't have to like it.

She had wanted him to put his arms around her and hold her and kiss her, not lay out the facts and push her at another man.

But sitting around crying about her lot in life wasn't going to fix anything. Torque wasn't being uncompassionate, he was being real. Intellectually, she knew it. But emotionally, she had to admit, it hurt. There was nothing easy about hearing the man you wanted with all your heart tell you to go find another man. But, for the last decade, at least, her life hadn't been about doing the easy thing. She couldn't let it become that now.

If she wanted her children, she needed to fight for them. And that's what she was going to do. Effective immediately.

"I'M SORRY. NEXT WEEK doesn't work for me. I had already made plans to move. I've taken off work, and there'll be boxes and other things lying around. So, see if the next week or the week after would work." Cassidy aimed her mouth toward where her phone lay on the table on speaker, while she spooned baby cereal into Nessa's mouth.

Her second call would be to her boss at the county courthouse taking next week off. She had no idea where they were moving to, but that was her plan. Even if it were a temporary place.

After the phone call to her boss, Cassidy called Torque. She wasn't really expecting him to answer, so she was surprised to hear his deep voice. "Cassidy?"

"I'm looking for a place to live. Something nice with a big yard for the kids. Money isn't an object. Can you set your minions on that?"

He didn't even snort. "I'll call Turbo as soon as I hang up. Is that it?"

"I need it next week."

Fifteen seconds of silence. Then, "Did you get kicked out?"

"Nope. I postponed the couple's visit with the twins by telling the adoption agency that I'm moving next week."

"So you're turning your lie into truth?"

"I guess you could say that."

"Okay. I started early 'cause I'm expecting the kids this afternoon."

"You know, if you were a bigger jerk, you would make this a lot easier for me."

More silence. "That it?"

"Yes."

He hung up. She had to laugh. He aimed to please.

After work, she pulled into the garage feeling like she had enough equipment to set up a fully equipped day care for a hundred kids.

Jamal jumped out of the car and went running to find Torque. Cassidy left the twins in their seats and lugged one of the heavy pack-n-plays to the knitting corner where two new ladies had joined the ladies she met yesterday.

"Cassidy, good to see you again," Gram said, setting her quilting down and standing.

"It's okay, you don't have to get up," Cassidy said, setting the heavy bundle down and starting to unstrap it.

"Where's that grandson of mine? Why isn't he helping you?"

Probably because I told him to be a jerk. Cassidy shrugged.

"I was wiping my hands so I didn't get grease all over everything." Torque came over and set the second play yard down. "I'll set 'em up. You get the babies."

"I can't wait." Miss Angelina rubbed her hands together.

Gram used her cane to come up beside Cassidy. She held her arms out, enveloping Cassidy in a warm, cinnamon-scented hug. "Thank you so much for bringing your children. We had such a good time watching Jamal yesterday. He reminded me so much of Torque when he was young."

Cassidy squeezed her back. She'd never been thanked for "allowing" someone to watch her children.

"This is Miss Alda." Gram pointed to one of the new ladies. "She never had kids, so we won't let her get too close."

"I watched my nieces and nephews, and I was their favorite auntie," Miss Alda said in a voice that sounded much younger than she looked.

Gram snorted. She whispered, "Don't worry. We'll still watch her."

"And I'm Beulah." An extremely short old woman with sparkling hazel eyes held her arms out. Cassidy was consumed in another hug. This one smelled like yeasty rolls, fresh from the oven.

"It's nice to meet you."

"I've heard a lot about you and that little boy of yours. Now, go get those babies so I can see them." Miss Beulah's eyes twinkled, and she looked beyond Cassidy's shoulder as though searching for the twins.

"Yes, ma'am." Cassidy was tempted to salute before she turned. She glimpsed a quirking of Torque's lip as she walked away, but she didn't stop to share a smile with him. She shouldn't have doubted that he would continue to be a gentleman, even though she had demanded he be a jerk.

She brought Nissa in, introduced her to the ladies, and set her in the play yard Torque already had set up. She'd just done the same with Nessa when her phone rang with a number she didn't recognize.

"Hello?"

Torque's eyes shot to her from where he stood on the other side of the play yard beside his gram and Miss Beulah. His expression was unreadable. She turned away.

"Hello. Is this Cassidy Kimball?" The voice was cultured and confident.

"Yes, sir."

"Cassidy, this is Brent Houser. Turbo Baxter gave me your number after I complained about my abject failure as an online dater."

Cassidy glanced at her kids, making sure they were okay, before she walked out of the garage, fighting for each step, like she was walking uphill underwater.

She tried to infuse friendliness and excitement into her tone. "You must be the orthopedic surgeon I heard so many good things about."

He chuckled. "I didn't want to lead with that. Sometimes it's intimidating."

At least he was a little humble. She could do this. She squared her shoulders and chatted with him a little, saying yes when he asked if she was interested in going out for dinner Saturday night. They hung up after agreeing on a time to eat and catch a movie.

Cassidy punched the button on her phone and allowed her hand to drop to her side. She stood with her back to the garage and her head down, trying to come to grips with what she'd just agreed to do. A date. That's all it was. And Brent seemed like a really nice guy. From what Turbo had implied, he was willing to be her savior. She was doing this for her kids.

But it didn't feel good or right.

She fingered her phone, unwilling to second-guess. If this was the path she'd chosen, she needed to walk down it, unwavering.

Lifting her chin, she shoved her phone back into her purse and turned.

Torque stood, leaning against the open garage door, the warm October sun casting his face into shadow under his ball cap.

She paused. "It was the doctor."

"Figured." He didn't move. One hand shoved in his pocket, one shoulder against the doorjamb.

"We're going out Saturday night."

"Good."

"He wants to meet the kids."

Torque nodded.

"He's picking me up."

His bicep twitched. "Gram and the ladies will help if you need a sitter."

"Okay." Implied behind his words was the thought that it wouldn't be the best thing for anyone if Torque were the ones watching her kids when Brent showed up to pick her up and drop her off. "That'd be nice if they could because I just remembered that Kelly is opening her first children's center across town and Harris will be helping her." Those were her go-to babysitters. She still hadn't recovered from the nanny episode enough to try to trust anyone she didn't personally know to watch her children.

Torque jerked his head. His face remained mostly hidden and completely stoic. She supposed that's how he survived the past ten years.

"Well, guess I'll go say goodbye to the kids."

He didn't move, and she started to brush by him.

"I'll quit a little earlier tonight, get supper, and get Jamal started on his homework."

"Thanks," she said, pausing in her walk before walking into the garage.

PUSHING THE DOOR TO her apartment open, Cassidy walked in on aching feet. It had been a discouraging evening. One property had no backyard; one was very nice but wasn't available for two months;

and one was perfect, except as she was leaving she saw her would-be neighbors in their backyard, the man flipping burgers and the woman with a wineglass in one hand and handing him a plate with her other one. Very friendly, since they both smiled and waved. Neither of them had a stitch of clothing on. She wouldn't be making an offer on that property until she researched the local zoning laws on how high and opaque property owners were allowed to make their fences.

She closed the door and leaned against it, never tiring of the sight of Torque, big and dark, and looking just a little dangerous, sitting at her table feeding her children. The big hands gentle, the easy answers in a deep, low voice to Jamal's questions as he chattered away. The adorable way the little girls gurgled and cooed and chattered in baby speak to him. The cozy feel of family in her kitchen. Torque didn't act like being with her children was an inconvenience or a problem. He might be a little awkward at times, but he never seemed irritated or like he wanted to be somewhere else.

Basically, it wasn't hard to picture this scene as her family.

But that was a mirage.

She pushed away from the door, and Jamal spotted her. "Mom!" He hopped up and ran to her, throwing his arms around her and chattering about his afternoon at the garage. The twins looked around and started bouncing in their seats, reaching out for her.

There was something about the smile of a baby and the innocence of a child. And the love of both. It might be a ratty apartment, small and old, but stepping into it gave her a warm, comforting feeling deep in her soul. There was no place in the world she'd rather be than with these souls right here.

Torque stood and turned. His face was impassive. "Jamal's homework's done. The twins just need baths. I set a plate of food on the stove for you under that cover. I'll clear the table before I go."

"Thanks," she said in a husky tone through the tightness in her throat.

He jerked his chin and gathered up the children's plates.

Jamal didn't know she was looking to move, so she didn't tell Torque about the houses and he didn't ask.

Torque finished clearing off the table and washed the few dishes. Drying his hands, he walked to the door.

Cassidy straightened from setting Nessa on the floor. "Do you mind if Jamal goes to the garage after school tomorrow?" She glanced at where the boy played on the floor with Nissa and lowered her voice. "I don't know how much more he'll be able to go..." She trailed off. Brent probably wouldn't want her son spending time with Torque. It probably wasn't wise anyway.

"He's welcome anytime," Torque said without turning around. His shoulders lifted and lowered like he was taking a deep breath. "You know that."

"Are you leaving?" Jamal ran over, grabbing Torque around the waist. "Don't leave. I wanted you to read my story tonight."

Torque bent down on one knee. Jamal threw his arms around him, crying that he couldn't go. His antics upset the twins who toddled over after him. They started crying too. Nessa crawled up on Torque's knee. Nissa leaned against his side.

Her happy home had transformed into chaos that fast. Cassidy bit back tears herself.

"I think it's best for me to go," Torque said, although Cassidy could hardly hear him over the din.

"No! Mommy, tell him to stay. He can't leave," Jamal wailed.

The neighbors were going to think they were torturing her children. In this neighborhood, she wasn't as concerned about them calling the cops as much as she worried they might knock on the door and ask to join in.

Torque's eyes lifted to hers. She bit her lip and shrugged one shoulder. She wanted him to stay, but she wasn't asking for it. He'd already done enough. Asking him to stay would only make things harder on him in the long run.

She went over and picked up Nissa.

"I'll stay." Torque pulled Jamal close and hugged him. Jamal clung to his neck like if he let go Torque might change his mind.

Guilt stabbed through Cassidy. She hadn't realized how much her little boy might be missing a father figure in his life. She'd selfishly thought that she was doing a good thing by giving him a home, but she couldn't be a dad, and he didn't need to tell her about it. He'd just shown her.

Chapter 19

Thursday went the same with Cassidy dropping Jamal off at the garage after school. Friday, she looked at more houses, and the Kicking Quilters helped Torque with the twins until he closed for the evening. He could hardly stand to think about the upcoming date on Saturday, and he wondered if he should pack up and move to a different town. Even the thought of Cassidy with someone else, despite knowing it was necessary, made his lungs feel like they were full of cement.

It almost took his mind completely off his own problems of not having the money he needed to make the down payment on renting the shop.

Until Friday afternoon, when two things happened.

The first thing was good.

Bob Smith brought his 359 Peterbilt in on the hook. "I'll pay you cash if you have it done by Saturday evening. I have a load that needs to be in California by Wednesday morning."

"I'll have to see if I can get the pistons cut and a rebuild kit from CAT."

Bless Cassidy and his new phone. He was able to make all the arrangements. This would easily tip him over the edge from having almost enough to make the down payments to having enough to not only secure his garage location, but he could go pickup shopping—something old and cheap—and would have all his parts bills for the week paid up as well.

Torque allowed himself a three-second smile before he got to work. He'd still be able to help Cassidy with the kids this evening and put Jamal to bed, but if the truck were going to be done by tomorrow evening, he wasn't going to sleep tonight.

Thankfully the Kicking Quilters were on with the twins. Since the next day was Saturday, Jamal didn't need to get up for school, so Torque didn't worry about quitting early. It was eight when Jamal, who was the official keeper of Torque's phone when he was there, said that his mom texted that she was on her way home.

Torque didn't bother to clean the shop, but he did wash his hands. Unlike the other nights, he dropped his gram off after taking Miss Angelina home but didn't take a shower or change.

"Why not?" Jamal said, when Torque just walked his gram to her door and said he wasn't going in.

"Going back to the shop to finish that motor soon as I get you settled in bed." He grinned.

Jamal's brows furrowed, and he gave Torque's dirty t-shirt an uncertain look, but he didn't argue when they drove his gram's car to the apartment.

Cassidy had a pizza on the table when Torque walked in behind Jamal, a twin in each arm.

"Oh my." She looked at his filthy outfit and her pretty pink daughters in his arms.

They'd settled into a stiff but friendly compromise, and Torque tilted his mouth. "I'm trying to keep them from touching me, but I'm heading back to the shop, so I didn't change."

"That's fine, of course. You can eat and run, if you need to."

"No!" Jamal said firmly.

Torque shrugged. "I can spare an hour. But I have a motor job that will let me pay the first and last months' rent, and the shop will be mine if I can keep it."

Cassidy froze in the act of taking Nissa out his arms. "That's what you needed? That's why you weren't sure you had the shop for more than a week? You had to have money for the down payment?" Her brows lowered, and her lips were pulled down.

Torque stared right into her eyes. Her anger wouldn't intimidate him. "Yes."

Her teeth ground together. He smiled. Honestly, if she hadn't been holding the baby, he thought she might have laid off and socked it to him. Maybe he deserved it for being such an arrogant, prideful s.o.b., but he felt so happy, he could float. Except the person he most wanted to share his almost-success with was going out on a date with another man tomorrow.

That thought brought him back down to earth, and he realized that he'd lifted his free hand and almost had it around Cassidy, wanting to bring her to him and kiss her full on the lips with God and everyone watching.

He swallowed, the smile fading from his mouth, and set the twin he held down on the floor.

Cassidy's lips compressed even more. "Wash up and sit down. We'll eat."

While he was washing his hands, Jamal ran to his bedroom to put his school things away.

"Did you find a house?" Torque asked low, after checking to be sure Jamal was still gone.

Cassidy's eyes lit up. "I did!" She, too, glanced at the hall doorway before saying in a low tone, "It has a huge front and backyard. A swing set already installed, six bedrooms, which we don't need, and it's beautiful, inside and out. Well back away from the road, no neighbors, and in a more affluent area, but not too ritzy for kids. It's also empty, and the owners are eager to close." She lowered her voice even more. "I told my agent to get it. Of course, it's Friday, and I probably won't know anything until Monday, but I could actually be packing next week." Her smile wrenched at his heart, but he had to smile back.

"I'm happy to hear it." That was his sincere truth. Once more, his body moved to kiss her before his mind shut it down.

Jamal came back out, and they settled around the table.

He'd barely taken one bite when his phone buzzed in his pocket. Taking it out, he glanced at the id. Miss Angelina. Had she fallen? Was she sick?

"I'd better get this. It's Miss Angelina."

Cassidy nodded.

"Hello?" Torque stood and walked away from the table.

"Torque, I'm sorry for bothering you." Her voice was breathless, like she had been running or maybe was nervous. "But I just received a call from my mortgage lender, and I wanted to tell you first. I didn't realize that when Tyke got the mortgage for this place that it was what is called a balloon mortgage. Have you ever heard of something like that?"

Torque leaned against the hall doorway. "You have a bunch of small payments then one big, massive payment at the end?" A buzz, like the sound a turbo makes just before it flies apart, started in his ears. His stomach muscles contracted.

"That's right. I didn't realize that's what it was, and the big payment, the massive one, was due last week." She paused. Torque tried to gather his thoughts, but he couldn't figure out which of the many questions spinning through his head he should ask first.

"I'm sorry, Torque." Her voice broke. She cleared her throat and went on. "But I don't have the cash to pay that payment. My daughters have some money, but I could never ask them to put it out for me." Her voice rambled on like she couldn't stop unloading her problems. "The banker suggested I sell. I thought I could keep my home if I had you there with the rent, but this is something I didn't expect, and I don't know what else to do." Her voice faded completely, and she sniffed.

Torque felt like a motor had just landed on his chest, but it hurt even worse to hear Miss Angelina, who was usually so happy and upbeat, crying in misery.

He shoved the panic back down and forced his brain to concentrate. "How long do you have?"

She sniffed and sobbed for a moment, trying to get herself under control. "The banker said I should put it on the market immediately, because houses don't sell as fast in the winter and he could maybe wait sixty days, but no more before things got really bad for me. So, maybe six weeks. I don't know what to do."

"Okay. So we have two months." He made his tone gentle but sincere. "We'll figure something out."

Miss Angelina sniffed. "I just feel so bad because you just told me today that you'd be able to stay and..."

"Don't feel bad. You didn't know, and if this doesn't work out, we'll go somewhere else. And I'll help you as much as I can in the meantime."

He didn't ask how much her balloon payment was. It didn't really matter since he had barely scraped enough together to get the money he needed as a down payment. There was no way he could start a business and make enough to pay her balloon payment along with everything else he needed.

He spent a few more minutes on the phone with Miss Angelina, trying to reassure her. But the lady felt like her life had just dumped her out upside down in an unfriendly territory.

Finally, he said, "I'm coming back to the garage tonight. Why don't you come on down and we'll figure out some options?"

She agreed, and he ended the call.

Everyone else was done eating when he sat back down. Cassidy lifted her brows at him.

"Sorry about that," he said as he picked up his pizza.

"That was Miss Angelina?"

"Yeah." His appetite had disappeared. "She doesn't know what to do about her balloon mortgage."

"I see." Cassidy tapped her chin. "Miss Angelina doesn't want to sell?"

"Pretty sure not. I don't know if it's because change scares her or she just wants to live right there, where she's lived for fifty years."

"It's sad her kids wouldn't support that."

"She said she didn't want to ask her daughters for money. I got the feeling at other times that the one lived pretty far away and the other didn't make that much. I don't know. Haven't seen 'em around. They were older than us. Like twenty years or so. I don't even know their names." He shoved pizza in his mouth without even tasting it. It didn't escape his notice that he and Cassidy were talking about his problems like an old married couple. If only. He probably shouldn't have burdened her with his issues. She had enough on her plate.

"Me either." Cassidy wiped Nissa and set her down. Nissa toddled over to Torque and raised her hands in the air.

"Want up, little one?" He reached down and set her on his knee, bouncing it, holding her with one hand while he ate with the other. She reached up with her hands and grabbed his face, squeezing before rubbing her fingers over his whiskers.

"I think she likes them." Cassidy smiled.

"So you like them, hmm?" he said to Nissa. "What does your mama think?"

She chortled and said, "Mama."

"Mama thinks he looks rakish and dangerous in his whiskers."

"Not sure if that was a compliment or not."

"It was." Cassidy got up and moved away.

Torque read to Jamal and slipped out of the apartment before Cassidy had the twins completely bathed and put down. He didn't want to overthink it, but it could be his last evening there, and he felt like he was leaving his heart with them. Gram had done her best, but nothing had ever felt quite so much like home as Cassidy's crummy apartment.

THAT WAS A BUST.

Cassidy closed the apartment door behind Brent. They never even made it to the movie.

He'd been great. Handsome. Successful. Seriously liked children. He'd even helped pack them in Gram's car, since the Kicking Quilters were taking them to Miss Angelina's home to watch them. They were going to bring them back to her apartment to put them to bed.

Cassidy checked the microwave clock. Five. She snorted. In another four hours, they would bring the kids home.

She could go get them. But she had to muster up the fortitude to face them after failing them so miserably.

The appetizer wasn't even on the table before she'd blurted out the truth to Brent. He'd been blindsided. Not about the kids; he already knew she needed someone who was interested in getting married, and soon, because of their potential adoption. But the other thing she'd blurted out. Heck, she'd surprised herself with what she said. However, she couldn't unsay it because it wasn't untrue.

Her cheeks felt hot, and she put her hands over them. She'd said to Brent something along the lines of, "It's only right to tell you that I'm in love with another man."

His chin had about hit the table. Hers almost landed right alongside of it.

Seriously? She was in love with Torque?

Well, yeah. How could she not be? How could any woman be on the receiving end of everything he'd done for her and not feel some kind of love? Even if he weren't the most handsome man she'd ever seen. Even if he didn't love her kids. Even if he wasn't resourceful and hardworking, honest and loyal. Kind. Tough. Strong. Compassionate.

Of course, she was in love with him. And, although she hadn't thought it out, it was only right to tell Brent.

He'd already had a love match with his late wife, he'd said, and he wouldn't stand in the way of her being with the one she loved. They'd left immediately, he'd dropped her off, and that was the end of it.

She'd ruined the one chance she had to give her kids an amazing dad that the adoption agency would be okay with.

Her heart beat slow, and she suddenly felt old and tired. Despair closed around her like a coffin lid snapping shut. What had she done?

Walking slowly to her bedroom, she fell onto her bed, facedown. She was going to lose everything she loved. The twins. Torque. Only Jamal was left, and she couldn't even provide the boy with the dad he deserved.

The kids were gone, and Cassidy indulged in a few tears.

Chapter 20

Torque locked the shop door behind him with bleary eyes. He'd not slept since five o' clock yesterday morning, and one would think that he'd be able to fall in bed and sleep 'til morning, but there was an irritation in his chest that he was pretty sure would keep him tossing and turning all night.

At least he'd been able to pay Miss Angelina. An hour ago when Bob left with his truck, Torque had gone immediately up to the house and presented her with the money he owed. He was officially in business. Now he needed to figure out what that meant. Tomorrow. Or next week. Sometime, but not tonight.

Tonight, he was going to take a walk.

He didn't even stop at the trailer to grab a jacket or change his clothes, just kept walking through the field, across the stream, and up the mountain. It was a hard climb—he lived on the steep, northern side—and he was out of breath by the time he reached the little lookout where he'd met Cassidy on the Fourth of July over ten years ago. He couldn't see the town, but the view was amazing. Especially this time of year with the trees turning and floating in twittering color to the ground. But he wasn't really watching that. He'd not been up here since that night. Man, he'd never imagined what he'd have to go through. The idea that he'd spend a decade behind bars had been nonexistent.

At that point in his life, he'd wanted two things—to be the best diesel mechanic around and to figure out how he could get Cassidy Kimball to marry him.

The second thing had seemed like an impossible dream. He knew she liked him, but the rich prom queen and private school grad who was going to Stanford wouldn't ever marry the poor boy from the trailer park.

A part of him thought it might have been possible now. If it weren't for her children and the mentoring program. She'd seemed to like kissing him okay.

But what had really driven him up the mountain tonight was the thought of Cassidy on a date with another man.

In prison, he'd assumed it was going to happen—she'd marry someone else and have their babies. But it hadn't been in his face. He'd closed himself off to any contact from her, thinking he wouldn't torture himself, sitting in his cell, wondering who she was with and what they were doing.

But it turned out she wasn't with anyone. Hadn't been doing anything. Did he flatter himself to think it might have been because of him?

Now, when he'd spent the last week remembering everything, falling in love with her children, falling in love with her, again...

He was in love with Cassidy Kimball.

Of course.

And that's what he wanted. Not her platitudes. Not her money. Not even her time. He'd wanted her love.

But he had to let that go. Just like he had to let the idea that had so recently taken hold—just this week after spending so much time with her and her family—that there might be a future for them together, he had to let it go.

She was with another man tonight. The thought sent hot fire through his blood, and he wanted to clench his fists and rail at the injustice of the universe.

A little voice whispered in his head that he had his garage. At least for now. He'd gotten half of what he wanted.

With all his heart, he knew for a certainty that he'd give up the garage, gladly, if he could have Cassidy.

He sat on the big rock that he and Cassidy had shared that hot July evening and watched the sunset fade from the sky.

"Torque?"

He jerked awake, glancing around, unsure where he was. Then it came back. The rock and the mountain. Although now, instead of sitting on the rock, he leaned against it, head back. One leg stretched out, one bent. His hand rested on his knee.

He blinked again. Someone had spoken. Sounded like Cassidy, only that must have been a dream because she was on a date with a doctor. Cassidy deserved a doctor.

"Torque? That's crap. I don't 'deserve' a doctor."

Had he said it out loud? He blinked and made out her outline against the sliver of moon behind her head.

He closed his eyes and leaned his head back. "Tell me he's not with you."

"He's not with me."

"You just saying that?"

"You told me to."

"Tell me the truth."

"He's not with me."

"Where are the kids?"

"Home in bed. Miss Beulah is holding down the apartment."

"Nice." He patted the ground beside him. "Sit down here and tell me about it. Must've been the best date ever, or it must have sucked, for you to be up here."

She settled beside him. "It sucked."

He tensed, and his eyes flew open. "Did he touch you?" There was going to be a dead doctor and a new body on death row if he did.

"No." She waved her hand in the air dismissively. It reflected the moonlight, and he grabbed it with his own, lacing their fingers together. Relishing the slide of her soft skin over his new blisters and old callouses.

"It was nothing like that," she said softly.

Relief eased through his body. "What, then?"

"He wasn't you," she said simply.

He shook his head, his heart hammering. "So that make two fools on this mountain."

"Torque." Her hand slid across his face where his stubble had turned into a two-day-old beard. "It's not foolish for me to love you."

His heart froze. His lungs collapsed. It was a good thing he was sitting down, since his entire body felt hot, then cold, then weak and trembly. How many years had he longed to hear that? How many dark, lonely nights in prison had he lain awake and thought that it would all be worth it if he had the love of his woman behind him? Her voice. Her image. Her scent. He could lie in his bunk at night and remember it all, every detail, until he almost shook with the need to hear those words.

Cold, lonely years, never-ending days, and empty nights. Hard cement. Bleak bars and a future he could never be sure of. All it took was Cassidy's love to make it worth it all. All the suffering. All the times he gritted his jaw and faced one more day. All the times he faced the gangs and the drugs and the fights. The abuse. The degradation. The loneliness. Being trapped. Everything.

His heart felt full. Like it could burst and rain down happiness.

If he hadn't been awake before, he was wide awake now. He shifted, taking her and settling her on his lap, looping his arms around her. She snuggled down, her head under his chin.

Cassidy loved him? No problems were insurmountable now. He felt invincible.

His voice came low and husky. He didn't even bother to try to hide the emotion in it. "I was sitting here tonight thinking about how much I loved you." He drew in a trembling breath. "And thinking about how much I wanted you to love me."

Her long, slender fingers cupped his bristled cheek. He leaned his head into her hand, needing to feel closer, wanting to pick her up, spin her around, and tell the whole world that this wonderful, amazing woman loved him.

Like she knew he needed to hear it again, she whispered, "I love you, Torque. That's what ruined my date. I told Brent it was only fair that he knew that I loved someone else."

He let out a trembling breath. "Scared him, huh?"

"He couldn't get me home fast enough." She laughed a little, her breath fresh and sweet against his face. "Really, he was nice. Perfect, actually. He'd have been a great dad. He was great with the kids when he met them. But he loved his first wife and said that if I loved someone, I shouldn't waste that precious gift."

"Just as perfect as I am imperfect?" Torque said. He'd meant it more as a statement, not looking for either a compliment or pity, but it came out of his mouth more like a question.

"You're perfectly imperfect."

"Except the adoption agency won't think so. Even if we could do something about the mentoring program." He ran his hand over her smooth hair. Every sensory receptor in his body sensitized by the new knowledge of her love. "You know, I realized tonight that despite my big words about working with my hands and all that crap..." He paused, sliding his hand down her back and up, fisting his fingers in her hair. "I realized I was full of BS. I'd give up the garage in a heartbeat if it meant I could have you."

Cassidy was quiet. "I want to say that I'd give up the girls to have you..."

"Shh." He placed a finger over her mouth. "Don't say it. Don't even think it. I won't let you make that choice. It's not a choice."

"Maybe it should be."

"No. I love you, and I feel like I'll be nothing without you. Can't even imagine it, but those babies need you." As full as his chest had just been, it now hurt. A searing, aching pain.

She lowered her head and said softly, "Tonight I just threw away my only chance to have them. Unless Turbo has some other poor sucker waiting in the wings."

His throat tightened, but he forced the words out. "Knowing Turbo, he probably does." Would he find out that Cassidy loved him, only to lose her immediately? The thought was almost inconceivable, but what other choice was there? He could never make her choose between the girls and him.

"That's the thing. The choice isn't even between giving you up or having the babies. I not only have to give you up, I have to replace you with someone else." Her hand crept around his waist. "I might be able to live without you. But I can never replace you."

He couldn't see any solution, and his elation of just a few minutes ago sank like cement blocks had hitched onto it. "I think we're at a dead end."

Cassidy was quiet before she said carefully, "So, I guess you go home to your side of the mountain, and I go home to mine?"

"Only we live on the same side, now." They laughed softly in the darkness.

"Ten years from now, we'll meet here again." She tilted her head up, and he gazed down at her, adding to her story.

"On July fourth."

"Yes, on July fourth."

"And we'll have the longest make-out session ever, since I've had you up here how many times now, and I've treated you like a lady every time." She loved him, and he at least wanted to kiss her. But he wanted to be able to back that kissing up with the ability to be there for her. Instead, he had to be gone.

The moon shone on her downturned lips. "I don't know why we need to wait ten years for that make-out session." She leaned closer. "What's stopping us tonight?"

"Because tomorrow, nothing's changed. I can't make out with a girl tonight and not make an honest woman of her tomorrow."

She huffed. "That's old-fashioned and a little chauvinistic, I think."

"I guess I'm old-fashioned and a little chauvinistic." But her lips were so close. The memory of their last kiss made his face tingle and his heart stumble.

She straightened in his lap and turned to face him. "Seriously? You're going to make me walk back down that mountain and face my mess of a life and I don't even get to make out with you first?" She placed both hands on his cheeks.

He should be strong. He should tell her no. She'd regret hurried kissing in the dark with a man who couldn't be there for her.

But she loved him, and he sure as heck loved her. Had for the last decade and then some. When she leaned closer, he met her halfway, their lips clinging. The embers that had been banked flared to life, higher and deeper because of the new knowledge, of the love that lay between them, acknowledged.

He pressed closer, pulling her toward him. It was real, finally, finally real. But, even as his heart hammered and his chest caught and burned, he knew it was only temporary.

Everything he'd ever wanted was just within reach, and he was losing it all.

CASSIDY SNUGGLED CLOSER, her lips still tingling from his kiss. She'd loved Torque for so long. Since way before he'd gone up for her. She couldn't even remember when her admiration for the quiet mechanic in town had morphed into love. But it didn't matter. Hearing from his lips tonight that he loved her made everything else so small in comparison.

"Cassidy?"

"Hmm?" His arms around her, his scent in the air, his heartbeat on her cheek. She was so content she could barely think. Nothing could make her happier.

"I did it because I loved you."

Except that.

She sat up. Her heart racing. His arms loosened, and he let her go. The moonlight put his eyes in shadow. She couldn't see, even though she searched. But her soul lifted, and her lips could only smile.

"I didn't know."

"Why else would I have done it? I can't believe you didn't know. When you asked me that, as I walked out of prison, it shocked me that you hadn't known. Hadn't thought I was the stupidest person in the world for sacrificing so much for a woman who barely knew I existed."

"I knew you existed. I had no idea how you felt about me." She cupped his face with her hands. "You're a good man, Torque. The best."

He shook his head. Her hands moved with it, brushing the roughness of his stubble, which sent shock waves up her arms.

"Not that good." His hands slid up her back. "I loved you then. I love you more now."

There was no way she could doubt it.

MONDAY MORNING, CASSIDY had just dropped Jamal off at school when her phone buzzed. She'd taken the week off work, the first whole week she'd actually taken since she started five years ago, and sat in the parking lot hoping it wasn't her boss calling to beg her to come in tomorrow.

It was the adoption agency.

"Hello?" Maybe they'd changed their minds.

"Miss Kimball. It's Anne Cargill. I know you told us that it didn't suit you to allow the twins to meet with the potential adoptive parents this week, but we really must insist."

"I'm sorry. I believe I told you I was moving."

"I understand. However, we are going to have to remove the girls from your home, if you cannot make them available to potential parents. This particular couple is threatening to go to another agency, and Nessa and Nissa could miss the opportunity to join their forever home." She sighed. "I know you love them, but you have to do what is best for them."

"I want the best for them. I actually meant to call you today. I have backed off my work schedule, and I'm moving into a new home." She hoped they accepted her offer.

"Thank you for telling me, Miss Kimball. I'm sorry, but my supervisor specifically said that in order for you to adopt Nissa and Nessa, there had to be a dad in the picture."

"Actually, there is."

"You found a husband that fast?" she asked skeptically.

"An old friend that I'd seen off and on recently moved back into town, and we've been seeing each other frequently. I did tell your supervisor that I had a serious boyfriend." Cassidy took a deep breath, she'd skirted the big lie, but she was about to jump in, might as well make as big a splash as possible. "He proposed last night. I accepted, and we're getting married in the next six months."

"That's great." If Anne suspected she was lying, she refrained from saying so. She did one better. "Bring him in sometime today, and he can fill out an application, and we can get him in the system."

Cassidy's heart stopped. "He works."

"I'll stay after. He can either come here tonight, or I'll call the potential adoptive parents and we'll meet you at your house at six."

She straightened her shoulders. It was time she faced the piper. "He'll be there today."

"I look forward to meeting him."

"I look forward to bringing him." Cassidy swiped off on her phone and dropped her head back against the headrest.

Thankfully there wasn't much going on at the office—there was always stuff to do—but Cassidy took off, driving to Miss Angelina's garage.

She had to admit to lying and to wanting to use him. He knew she loved him, but this was a major request. He might resent being her last option and choice. Her fingers shook as she slammed her car door shut.

She walked into the cool, dark interior and stopped, allowing her eyes to adjust. Straight back, several ladies sat on chairs. They called out a greeting, and she answered.

"Torque's over there under that truck," one of the ladies called. Cassidy took a hard right and walked around the back of a big rig. She'd been in the garage once, back when she'd been with Torque. The size of the rig impressed her. Made her feel small. Also made her impressed that Torque was as good as he was with them. She knew the wheels went on the ground. That was about it.

Torque's legs stuck out from under the truck in front of the drive tires where some clanging and banging echoed around the garage. "Torque?"

The clanging stopped. His legs stiffened. "Cassidy?"

"Do you have a minute?"

He rolled out from under the truck and stood in one smooth motion. "Is everything okay?" His brows furrowed, and he looked around the garage. "Where are the kids?"

"I left them in day care. I, uh..."

He grabbed a rag out of his pocket and started wiping his hands, walking toward her. "We can go to the office if you want."

"No." She swallowed. Her stomach felt like an out-of-control courtroom. "The adoption agency called today. I told them about all the changes I'm making, but it wasn't enough and I might have said that I would bring my boyfriend in this afternoon."

His hands stilled. His eyes widened then darkened. Then his lips flattened. "You want me?"

"Yes."

"They might reject me."

"It's possible. I've looked up the law. It doesn't say anything about convicts adopting, and since your 'crime' was technically with a vehicle, they probably would be okay with it. I just don't know about the recent release."

"We can try."

Cassidy closed her eyes in relief. She should have known Torque would come through for her. He always had.

"What time?"

Chapter 21

At noon, Cassidy walked into the adoption agency beside Torque. Anne greeted them and gave him an application to fill out. She left them in the waiting room. The scratch of Torque's pen was the only sound as Cassidy looked around at the cute pictures of happy families stuck to the bulletin board. Brown carpet, forgiving of the spills and splashes of babies and toddlers, covered the floor, and the walls were painted a neutral beige.

She tucked her feet under her chair to keep them from bouncing.

The scratching stopped.

He couldn't be finished. It was four pages long.

She lifted her brows.

"It asks flat out, 'Have you ever been arrested or served time in prison?'"

Cassidy's heart sank. She'd forgotten about that question. Funny how so many things were an automatic yes or no—with the questions not even registering.

Torque watched her with dark brown eyes, deep and true. He'd lie for her. All she had to do was ask. But that wasn't the kind of man he was, and he would never do it under any other circumstances.

"Tell the truth, please."

His white teeth flashed, contrasting with his natural tan. "Love you."

Her heart flipped. She'd never get tired of hearing that. "I love you, too."

He finished filling out the form and handed it to the receptionist. As he sat back down, he grabbed her hand, which made her smile again.

The clocked ticked slowly around, and fifteen minutes went by before Anne stuck her head out of her office door and called them back.

They hadn't even sat down before she spoke. "Mr. Baxter, you answered 'yes' to the question about being arrested and serving time in prison. Could you tell me what year that was, how long you were incarcerated, and how long you've been out?" She walked around her desk.

"It was ten years ago. I served ten years, and I've been out about ten days."

Anne blinked and looked up. "Ten days? You've been out of prison for ten days?"

"Yes, ma'am."

Cassidy's heart sank. She knew it was a long shot, with more chance of failure than success and the very real possibility of her embarrassing herself. Like she'd just done. But she had to try. She couldn't live the rest of her life, knowing that there had been something else she could have done but she didn't do it because she was afraid of failing or of looking like a fool. And Torque had agreed.

"You're on parole?"

"No, ma'am. I served my whole sentence."

"I see." She made a mark on the paper. "Cassidy, I'm sorry. We simply cannot allow those children to go to a home where one parent has been so recently incarcerated. I hope you understand." Her lips tilted down, and she truly did seem sorry.

"I understand. I hope you understand that I had to try."

Anne smiled. A friendly smile. "I've actually spoken to several people about you, including your boss, and I know you would make an excellent mother. I understand that you're moving and hiring a nanny and cutting your hours. I've seen Jamal and how much he wants to be with his sisters. I'm not heartless. I want those girls to be with you. But there's no way this," she indicated the application and Torque's recent prison stint, "will fly. It just won't." She tapped her pen on her desk. "But," she emphasized that word. "But I will throw this application away. I'm not mentioning it to anyone. So," she paused and lowered her voice, "if you were to happen to find another boyfriend that you've been seeing for a while and has just proposed marriage, I might be able to help you out. Not to marry him," she said quickly. "I don't want you entering into an unstable relationship, which would hurt the children, but just someone who can help you out until you get things under control. My supervisor might be convinced to allow you to adopt as a single mother with a steady boyfriend if you have several good home visits." She tilted her head, a small grimace of apology on her lips. "I'm saying, I can bend the rules that far, but I can't break them like this." She pointed to the ten days out that was circled in red ink.

"Thank you." Cassidy's lips felt like blocks of cement, but she forced them to work. "I appreciate it."

"I am headed out on vacation, but my supervisor, Larissa Rice, wants to bring our prospective couple out tomorrow evening." Her eyes dripped sympathy. "Let this happen. And in the meantime, do everything you've been working on, plus a steady father figure, and I'll work as hard as I can for you."

Cassidy nodded. There was no point in fighting it. "That's fine. There will be boxes scattered around, but we'll make do."

"Thank you."

Cassidy stood. Torque stood beside her. They shook hands with Anne and walked out together.

"I'm sorry," Torque said as soon as they stepped into the parking lot.

"It's not your fault. It's mine. And really, if you think about it, it serves me right. I'm still being punished for my fatal decision. I deserve it." Her neck felt like it was caught in a tight, pinching grip, and her feet seemed to drag on the ground.

Her phone buzzed, and she grabbed it with one hand.

"It's the realtor." And, even though she might not be sharing the house with the twins, a thrill still traveled down her spine. Jamal would love the new place.

She swiped with her thumb, unwilling to let go of Torque's hand. "Hello?"

"Cassidy. Glad I caught you. Unfortunately, I have bad news. There was another offer placed on the house last Friday, and the owners have accepted."

Cassidy had to laugh. Could the day get any worse? She looked over at Torque. She could lose him. That would make it worse. The thought chilled her.

She thanked her realtor and hung up, not even bothering to set up a new time to look at houses. She couldn't remember being more discouraged since Torque was sentenced.

TORQUE SLOUCHED IN his chair at the mentor meeting as Frank Bigelough called it to order and gave some opening statements and announcements. There were a few new pairs, and Frank had them introduce themselves.

Torque's heart pounded hard and slow in his chest. Cassidy wasn't going to like what he was about to do. He'd not talked to her about it because he knew she would hate the idea. But he'd talked to Turbo that afternoon, and he intended to do what needed to be done.

As he had at the last meeting, Frank had each pair report on their progress. When it was their turn to speak, Torque stood before Cassidy could open her mouth.

"I wanted to thank everyone for their support. I especially want to thank Miss Kimball for agreeing to mentor me. Unfortunately, I'm going to have to drop out of the program because I've been offered a job in Alaska driving on the ice roads. It's good money, and I've accepted. I'm leaving next week. 'Preciate everyone's encouragement."

Torque sat as the folks around the table politely clapped. Beside him, Cassidy sat like an ice sculpture. He could feel waves of cold anger blowing off her. He deserved it for not discussing his decision with her. But he didn't want to go, and it had taken all his willpower to make the decision. If she tried to talk him out of it, he'd cave immediately. He knew he would.

"Maybe Miss Kimball will volunteer to be a mentor to another ex-con." Frank smiled encouragingly.

"Maybe," Cassidy agreed with a distinct lack of enthusiasm.

Frank moved on to the next pair.

Cassidy glanced at him once, her mouth flat, her eyes spitting fire. He smiled, because he knew it would make her even more angry. He could face the inevitable confrontation better with her anger than with any other emotion she could display.

The meeting dragged. Cassidy sat stiffly beside him. He didn't pay any attention to anything else that happened. The pain in his chest made it difficult to even breathe.

When it finally left out, Cassidy and he walked out immediately.

The door had barely shut behind him before she said, "What was that about?"

"It's true. Even before I got out of prison, Turbo had mentioned the Alaskan ice roads. He put my app in, and once my license came back, they called. I can start as soon as I can get there."

Cassidy had stopped in the dark parking lot. "You're kidding."

Her eyes blazed, her hair blew in the breeze. Slender and regal, she looked like a queen standing there. So far above him, and yet she loved him. Well, he loved her too. And this wasn't the first time he'd made a sacrifice because he loved her. That thought strengthened his resolve, and he spoke, his voice firm. "No."

She looked around, her mouth opening and closing, but no sound coming out. "I thought...I thought..." Her voice broke, and her eyes started to fill.

Torque's heart lurched. He couldn't do this if she cried. He knew he couldn't.

Her jaw clenched, and she whispered fiercely through it. "I thought you loved me."

"I do." He looked over her shoulder. He couldn't look into her eyes filled with tears. "Listen, you heard the lady at the adoption agency. She said you still had a chance. Turbo found another prospect, and this one actually sounds better than the last. Your friend Kelly knows him too. But I need to go. This opportunity came up, and I knew if I was out of the way, things would work out for you."

Cassidy put a hand up. "Couldn't we have talked about it?"

His chest felt hollow. "Maybe I should have."

"What about the garage?"

"She's selling the place." He reminded her about the balloon mortgage. "I'm going to have to leave anyway."

"She's selling the garage?"

Another dream that was so close, and yet, he lost it too. "And the house. It's all on one deed."

Cassidy folded her arms across her chest and stuck her chin out. "Torque, this is just like what you did when you sent me off at the accident. You can't make decisions that you think are best for me then just order me around. You can't be the one to make all the sacrifice."

He was quiet, his heart beating painfully. Then and now. The reasons were the same.

He took a breath. "Then choose, Cassidy. I'll stay if you want, but you're going to lose the twins. Jamal will lose the opportunity to know his sisters, and you'll have to look at me every day for the rest of our lives knowing that it was all my fault. Or I can go. You can get the babies, and you might end up with a really great husband."

"That's not you."

He lifted a shoulder, not trusting himself to speak. "But you have to understand, I can't stay and watch that."

He could see understanding dawn across her face. "I get it. It would hurt far more for me to watch you be with another woman than for me to have to be with someone I don't love."

He shoved his hands in his pockets. Other people had started to come out of the building, but they were far enough away that he could only see, not hear, them. Meeting Cassidy's gaze, he tried to hide the searing pain in his heart and chest. Did blood burn like oil? It felt like it.

"I see your point." She bit her lip, then she smiled a little, like she realized he wasn't changing his mind and she didn't want their last conversation to be only fighting. "I guess we get to say goodbye this time."

His heart sank. "I guess."

"When are you leaving?"

"I have enough work I've promised to do to finish out this week."

She swallowed. He appreciated her chin-up attitude.

"And you're not changing your mind?"

"No."

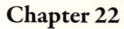

Chapter 22

Torque swept the garage floor. Little puffs of dust gathered above the pile of metal shavings and other debris that collected on the floor after a long day of changing brakes and drums and replacing a rocker arm.

Only one more day. He didn't want to get melancholy. Although the feeling that he'd had everything he'd ever wanted and it all was slipping through his fingers tightened his chest and made his stomach cold.

He'd been so close. So close to having Cassidy—who would have thought that she'd ever admit that she loved him? And so close to realizing his dream of opening his own garage.

He bumped the broom on the floor. Tyke had left his garage neat, and Torque would do no less. There was still tomorrow, but only about a half a day's work—rotating the tires on a trailer and fixing a wiring issue. Shouldn't take long.

He'd turned down so much work this week...

Shaking his head, he waited for Jamal to hold the dustpan in position. Even Jamal had been subdued today, barely talking, which was unusual.

In prison, he'd decided he wasn't looking back. Ever. All it did was make him sad and frustrated. Always look ahead and plan and prepare for the future. Driving the ice roads would be fun and exciting. Dangerous. Turbo said he might even come up for a few months. Alaska would be wild and beautiful, and who knew what opportunities would arise while he was there?

He leaned on the broom handle, watching Jamal walk the garbage to the can, looking around the garage. He was just fooling himself, and he knew it. Everything he ever wanted was right here in Pennsylvania, but there wasn't a darn thing he could do about it. He had no choice but to walk away.

The main door opened. An older woman with hair the color of strawberry ice cream walked in. Torque walked over, putting the broom away, figuring the woman must be lost.

"Hello, ma'am. Can I help you?"

"I'm looking for Torque Baxter."

"That's me." He stopped a yard or two from her, bracing his legs and folding his arms over his chest. Jamal came over and stood beside him. For once, saying nothing.

"I'm Angelina Ford's daughter."

Torque held out his hand. "Good to meet you." Miss Angelina had left earlier because her daughter was visiting. He waved a hand at Jamal. "This is my after-school help, Jamal."

"It's nice to meet you, Jamal," the woman said as she shook his hand. Her eyes squinted and her brow furrowed as she looked at the boy. She looked back at Torque and opened her mouth, but then, like she changed her mind, she closed it.

She straightened. "I was up at the house visiting my mother, and she couldn't stop talking about you. I wanted to come down and meet you." She looked Torque up and down. "I have to say, you don't look the way I thought you would. I thought you'd be older."

Torque shrugged.

"She said how you have these little kids running around and how you're patient with them and all that. But what I really wanted to thank you for was letting my mother come down here with her knitting group."

Torque jerked his head at the chairs. Tough had found two old recliners and dragged them in. "We were still looking for two or so more recliners. It's easier on the ladies' backs."

She walked slowly toward the area where the recliners were set up with a small table and an apartment-sized refrigerator. Torque had also set up a coffee maker on a shelf in the corner. "Wow, they have their own little place."

"When my mom died back when I was in elementary school, those ladies gave my brothers and me each a quilt. Guess I figured I was too old to cry, but I wasn't too old to ball up in that old quilt at night. Meant something to me."

"I see. Sounds like something Mom and her friends would have done." She tapped her cheek before drawing in a deep breath. "Well, I guess you know we're listing the property. Mom's too old to be here by herself, and I don't have time to watch her. I'm still working. But I just wanted to come down and meet you. Never heard of a mechanic that took the time to teach little kids in his shop and allowed old ladies to set up their quilting group." She looked at him full-on, her blue eyes an interesting contrast to her strawberry pink hair. "I work with children. So many are neglected and abused. I like what you're doing."

"Thanks," Torque said, even though his chest felt cold and empty. It was great for the short time it lasted.

She held out her hand. "I hope we meet again. The world needs more people like you."

TORQUE WALKED INTO Cassidy's apartment just a little after five with Jamal. Cassidy had supper ready to set on the table. It was their last meal together. He wasn't leaving until tomorrow, but he was heading out as soon as the last of the work was done.

Tonight would be the last time she'd see him. Unfortunately, the adoption agency had insisted that tonight the prospective adoptive parents would have their first supervised visit with the twins.

Cassidy had a dinner date scheduled with Turbo's prospective suitor tomorrow, and she'd been trying to psych herself into thinking that it was going to go well. But all she could really think was that tomorrow at this time, Torque would be gone.

The twins were already in their high chairs. She walked over as they came in, stooping to give Jamal a hug then sending him to his bedroom to put his backpack away. Standing, she put her arms around Torque. She didn't usually greet him like that, but since it was their last day...

He stiffened. All week it was like he was trying to pull himself away. She could understand. The less one cared, the easier it was to leave.

Then he relaxed under her touch, and his arms came around her, pulling her close. They stood for a while. When she started to back away, he leaned down and kissed her. Just a short kiss, but her knees still got weak, and her hands gripped his solid shoulders.

He lifted his head. "Hello."

She laughed, trying to push away the sadness, the thoughts of why couldn't this be her life? To just be in the present. Tomorrow would be soon enough to deal with the rest of her life.

They sat and ate, talking with each other and Jamal, both of them avoiding any mention of any topic that might remind them this was the last, or that he was leaving, or that she was going on a date with someone else tomorrow at this very time.

Time slipped away, and they were a little late cleaning the table. Cassidy had wanted Jamal to be done with his homework before their guests showed up, and Torque had planned to be gone. But Jamal still sat at the table, his math book open in front of him. Torque sat beside him, a twin in each arm. They'd taken to doing that—after she got them down from their high chairs, they toddled over to Torque for a cuddle on his lap before hopping down and waddling off to play.

The knock on the door surprised her. She hadn't realized it was that late, and they were ten minutes early. Her eyes widened, darting around the room, as though she were looking for a good hiding place. She met Torque's gaze. Calm. Relaxed. A little pain in the depths, but a calm acceptance foremost.

He bounced the babies and smiled at her. She made her lips tilt up in response then strode to the door.

Larissa Rice stood there in her pink hair, carrying her briefcase and clipboard. Beside her, a professional-looking couple in their late twenties looked eager and excited. The man seemed a tad apprehensive. But twins could be a handful, so that was probably a smart feeling.

They introduced and greeted each other, and Cassidy invited them in.

Mrs. Rice stopped dead still in the middle of the room. "You," she said.

Torque stopped his explanation of the lowest common denominator while leaning over Jamal's shoulder and glanced up. His eyes widened just a fraction, and his mouth twitched up.

Cassidy had to admire him. His hair still slightly wet from his shower, his white t-shirt contrasting against his own dark complexion and the dark hair and skin of Nessa and Nissa. The twins' pink outfits looked adorable against his bulging biceps. He stood gracefully. Their chubby arms went around his neck as they chattered to each other. Carrying them with familiar ease, he took a few steps and stopped beside Cassidy.

Her face must have shown her confusion. He said, "This is Miss Angelina's daughter. I just met her at the garage a couple of hours ago."

Cassidy's eyes widened. She looked at Larissa again. Miss Angelina's blue eyes looked back at her. "I didn't see the resemblance until just now."

Larissa looked down at her clipboard, then back up at Cassidy and Torque, then down and up again. Her mouth opened and closed. The couple beside her shifted.

Finally, she said, "Are you two...?" She motioned between Torque and Cassidy.

Torque didn't move. He was waiting for Cassidy to decide and answer. Cassidy went with her courtroom instincts.

She reached for Nissa, who leaned out of Torque's arms easily, and stood close to Torque. His arm came around her, and she leaned against him.

"Yes. We were good friends in high school." She looked up at Torque. "Maybe a little more than good friends. And I love him now."

Larissa glanced over at the couple beside her. They'd not said a word. "Would you excuse us for a moment?"

They exchanged a surprised look.

"If you'd just wait outside here for one minute." Larissa opened the door, and the confused couple stepped out.

She waited for them to go and said in a low tone, "Then why don't you marry him?"

"Because he was just recently released from prison."

"Oh." Her eyes hardened. "What was he in for?"

"Vehicular homicide. He was only seventeen, but they gave him a ten-year sentence, and someone made sure he served every day of it."

Her brow puckered. "I remember Dad talking about..." She drilled Torque with her eyes. "Did you win the truck pull at the county fair before you went to prison?"

"Twice," Torque said.

"I remember Dad talking about how harsh your sentence was. He couldn't figure out why, since he said you were a good kid." She tapped her cheek for long moments. For once, the twins were quiet and still, as if they knew their fate hung in the balance.

Finally, Larissa's hand dropped. "If I recall correctly, the only reason you were denied permission to adopt the girls is because you were a single mom and we thought it was too much for you, especially since you already have an adopted son. Is that right?"

"That's correct," Cassidy confirmed. "And I tried to apply with Torque, but we were denied because of his prison record and recent release."

Larissa stared off into space for several moments. Finally, she jerked her clipboard up and began writing furiously. "Well, I just changed that decision. If you still want to adopt these girls, you are approved. Right there is the kind of man we want for a dad. My mom couldn't say enough good about him, and I just visited him at work, where I found everything she had said to be completely true."

Cassidy's mind reeled, and her head spun. Torque's arm tightened around her. "You're saying the girls are ours?"

"That's exactly what I'm saying." She gave a decisive nod before cringing a little and looking at the closed door. "This isn't the most professional way to handle this, but this agency is all about the children, finding good homes and parents who will love them and raise them well. That's what is going to happen here." She opened her eyes wide and shook her head. "I've never done anything like this before, but I've never been more sure of anything in my life. We'll finalize the adoption as soon as you finalize your marriage."

Cassidy let out an excited squeal and took one hop before she froze and checked out how Torque was taking this.

She needn't have worried. He was smiling. "Guess I'd better go ring shopping."

"I don't need a ring. I just need you."

He pulled her closer and lowered his head, kissing her sweetly.

Epilogue

Cassidy stood in Miss Angelina's big yard, her hands on her hips. Actually, it wasn't Miss Angelina's big yard anymore. It was hers. Torque's and hers.

She twisted the small diamond on her hand. Their wedding was a few short weeks away. Nothing fancy. Despite her privileged upbringing, they weren't the showy kind of people. Plus, planning a wedding while trying to move and settle three children into a new home all while working part-time was more than either of them wanted to do.

Torque had allowed her to move in with the kids first. But he was there every day, of course.

Cassidy laughed as Torque caught one of the twins as they raced down the yard. He picked her up and spun her around. He took three steps to where Jamal had his bike in pieces on the blacktop.

"Looks good, son. I'll help you take a link out of that chain as soon as you get it off."

He probably should have done it in the garage and would have for sure, if he'd thought about it. Cassidy figured he was just in such a big rush to be just like Torque—his dad. The adoption papers came through yesterday for Torque and Jamal.

They were waiting until they were married to officially adopt the girls. But everything was lined up and ready to go.

Torque set the twin down and walked the twenty yards back up to her, where she stood beside Nessa in the play yard.

"Still sleeping?" he asked softly.

"Yes." Cassidy smiled as he strode confidently to her and pulled her close.

He looked up at the house before he turned and stood with his arm around her. "If you'd told me last year this time, while I was sitting behind bars feeling sorry for myself, that this would be my life, I'd have thought you were the biggest liar I'd ever met."

"I can't believe it either."

Miss Angelina caught Nissa as she toddled to the blacktop. Gram and Miss Betty laughed from their chairs where they quilted outside the garage. It was a beautiful Sunday afternoon, and the garage was closed up for the day.

"Do you think Miss Angelina minded moving to the mother-in-law suit in the west wing of the house?" Cassidy lay her head on Torque's shoulder.

"Not at all. She told me that's the reason she and Tyke built that suite—for them to eventually move into. I thought you were there when she said it."

"I might have been. Sometimes I miss things when the twins are talking. I'll never get tired of hearing them call me 'mama.'"

"And you're a good mama. The very best." Torque's arm tightened around her.

"Okay. *Dad*."

Torque's teeth flashed white in his tanned face. "You can call me that all day."

She laughed. "You know, I thought I saw Tough looking at Kelly the other day when she was here at the house and he was at the garage helping you with that big motor job."

"Really?"

"Yeah. He was standing in the garage door, looking up here. I couldn't see his face or anything, but Tough isn't usually distracted."

"True. He wasn't distracted for long. I never saw him stop working." He shook his head and put his hands on her shoulders, turning her to face him. "It doesn't matter anyway. Kelly has that rich politician she's with, and I honestly don't think Tough will ever get married. He'd have to actually ask a question. To a girl." He laughed. "Tough's great, but nope. Don't see him getting married."

She laughed with him, although she wasn't sure he was correct. Tough wouldn't need to talk. Kelly could speak for both of them.

"Now, about our wedding. What do you say we move it up?" His eyes darkened as his head lowered. "Like tomorrow? This afternoon, even?"

"Okay," she whispered as his lips touched hers. Getting married was a big decision, but with Torque, she wasn't afraid, wasn't even nervous. How could she be? After what he did, she was ready to do whatever he wanted.

The End.

Thanks so much for reading! Click here[1] to sign up for my Reader Group News to get exclusive deals, offers and information on me and my writing!

Keep reading for a sneak peak at Tough's story, *Tough Talk*, available January 22, 2019.

---

1. http://jessiegussman.com/subscribe/

Tough Talk Sneak Peak

Chapter 1

Tough clicked "publish" and allowed a small smile to hover on the corners of his lips. Funny how the words that never came easily out of his mouth flowed without effort from his fingers.

Placing his hands behind his head and leaning back with a loud squeak from the ancient, wobbling office chair, he allowed himself a grunt of satisfaction as his phone began chiming with notifications.

He had just reached to shut his computer screen off when a squeal and crash shook the walls of the old warehouse. His chair's legs slapped back down on the concrete. He jumped to his feet and strode out of the office, through the cavernous, cement-floor interior that he used as his garage. He past the now-deserted checker board where retirees sat during the day while he worked on customers' cars and grabbed the knob of the side door. The warehouse wasn't exactly square, and the old metal door always required a good jerk to slip it out of its frame.

Tough yanked. The door flew open.

Just off the sidewalk in front of his building, an older model car with minimal front end damage sat beside a light colored hybrid. The damage to the hybrid was heavier, but still not extensive. According to the placement of the cars, it looked like the older one cut the corner too close and clipped the hybrid as it sat at the stop sign.

Tough's heart did a light stumble as he recognized the perky little blond who had jumped out of her car and was walking around. Kelly Irwin. Her face scrunched up as though in pain when she saw the damage to her car. But she didn't stop, continuing to the driver's side of the other vehicle.

He glanced in the window of her car. Normally she had at least two underprivileged children with her anywhere she went outside of her job as a social work supervisor. Not today.

Tough didn't see anyone else in the other car, either.

The older gentleman had gotten out, meeting Kelly over his door.

Kelly lifted a hand to keep long strands of honey blond hair out of her face as a breeze tunneled down between the two large buildings on either side of the street. "Are you okay?" She let go of her hair and touched the man's arm.

He rubbed his head. "I'm fine. I can't believe how much damage there is. I wasn't going that fast!"

She smiled reassuringly at him, her whole face lighting up, and patted his arm. "I know you weren't." She held her hand out. "I'm Kelly, by the way."

"Grant Hormel." The man shook her hand, but the worry lines never eased from his face.

Tough considered the damages and figured it was true; they really weren't going very fast. It might look like a lot, but really, the he damage was minimal. Easily fixed in his shop where he did body and motor work.

At this point, Tough knew, any "normal" person would have walked over with their hand out. They'd introduce themselves and mention the auto body shop they owned just behind them. They'd mention that their shop had just emptied out this morning. They'd offer to give an estimate, get the car in and have it fixed by closing tonight.

Tough clenched his jaw. His eye twitched. Unfortunately, his unusual name was the most normal thing about him. Always had been.

Kelly opened her mouth, but the man spoke again. "I'm so sorry. I dropped my phone and I just leaned over to pick it up and that's when…"

"Yes, it's okay," Kelly said gently. "I know these happen so fast. Please don't feel bad. Nobody was hurt. That's the important thing. The cars can be fixed." She patted his arm.

The man twisted his hands together and took a shaky breath. "I hate to ask this of you, but could we keep from reporting this? My kids have been trying to take my license from me for a year now, and once I lose it..."

Kelly's hand stayed consolingly on the man's arm, and his hands quit twisting together. "Hey. It's okay. I understand. It could have happened to anyone. We don't have to report this."

"Really?" The man looked like he was going to hug Kelly. But then his face fell. "I won't be able to pay for your repairs up front. I'm on social security. But I can do payments."

"Let's take it one step at a time." Kelly shifted and looked at the front of the man's car. "I think your car will be fine. Her face tightened when she looked at her own. "Mine, not so much. I don't know how much that will cost." Kelly held up the phone in her hand. "I can Google body shops."

Tough leaned out toward the street and looked up at the admittedly battered homemade sign above his door. "*Tough Bodywork*." He'd deliberately not put an apostrophe "s" on the end of his name. Enough people had ribbed him about the idiotic names his father had given him and his brothers before his dad split for good. He'd decided he might as well make a play on it himself when he named his shop.

The name wasn't the only thing he'd been made fun of for over the years. He'd learned a long time ago it was better to twist life to suit him, than to wait for others to twist it to hurt him.

He straightened and looked back out on the street, at the cars that were less than ten feet from him. At the people who were not much farther away. How was he always invisible to flesh and blood humans?

He cleared his throat.

WHAT HE WANTS

The man shifted nervously. Kelly's fingers flew over her phone. The bright red nail polish glinted and flashed. The earrings dangling at her lobes clinked. The woman was never still and seldom quiet.

A tight little ball formed in the back of Tough's throat. He swallowed it away. It didn't bother him at all that most people didn't notice him. He actually preferred it that way. It did bother him some that Kelly seemed to be the same as most people, at least in that area.

"Oh, it says that there's one real close to here." Kelly's brows furrowed as she looked up, around and behind her at the building across the street.

Tough crossed his arms over his chest and leaned against the wall. *Not there, Kelly.*

She looked back down at her phone and tilted her head, as though trying to figure out which way to read the map.

So he stood watching as Kelly made a slow turn, her white and blue dress puffing out in the breeze, looking up and down the dilapidated buildings at the end of the street.

Tough's heart pumped harder, faster as her gaze moved closer. She saw the sign first. She glanced at her phone, then back to the sign. A smile tugged up the ends of her lips. His heart stumbled. Her gaze swept down the building. Her eyes widened as they landed on him.

His eye twitched and the muscle in his jaw bunched. He didn't even try to swallow the lump in his throat. From past experience he knew he'd never be able to speak around it anyway. He had always been tongue tied with strangers, and women in particular. He came out of the womb that way. Unfortunately.

He could talk cars, so he'd never had a problem in his shop, until a customer started talking about the weather or the ball game, or, God forbid, something more personal.

Sparkling white teeth flashed in Kelly's perfectly tanned face. Her dress swooshed around her legs as she hurried toward him, her hazel eyes bright and clear, polite enquiry on her face.

"Excuse me, sir. Could you tell me if the auto body shop behind you is open?"

"Yeah." Tough managed to get one word past the log jam in his throat.

Kelly paused, as though waiting for him to say more. When he didn't her pink lips pursed, then she smiled even brighter.

"So, is it, or isn't it?" She spoke slower, the way many people did when they talked to him.

His chest burned a little.

"Yeah," he said again. That word, and "no," were the two words he knew he could almost always get past his closed up throat. They were sufficient in most situations.

"Okay, great. Then I'll just head inside and talk to the owner." She started to brush past him.

He forced his mouth open. "That's me."

She stopped so fast her sandals almost left skid marks on the sidewalk. Spinning around, her dress billowed out, brushing his jeans, reminding him of his air brush with its light touch and attention to detail. Only it made his leg hot, like a welding burn. Her perfume flirted with his nose. He breathed deep to catch its full-bodied flavor. It was the smell of money with sunshine and glitter. Her hair shimmered like wet paint in the sun.

Her eyes met his, but he couldn't stand the intimacy and his gaze skidded over her shoulder to the peeling metal behind her.

"I'm sorry, Mr.—" she looked down at her phone. "—Baxter." Her head snapped up. "Hey, you're Torque's brother."

Tough jerked his head up in agreement. Yep. He was. Torque's brother.

"I didn't know your shop was here."

"It is." He cursed his stupid tongue that knotted every time he tried to use it.

"Well, that's just great." She held her hand out. "I'm Kelly."

He knew her.

"My best friend, Cassidy, is marrying your brother."

Knew that too.

He held his dirty hands up, to show her he wasn't being rude by not shaking her outstretched hand.

She grabbed his hand as he raised it and pumped it anyway. "I've heard so much about you," she said, her smile bigger and brighter up close. "I think we've been that close," she held up two fingers about an inch apart, "to meeting several times over the last six months since Torque got out of prison..." her voice trailed off like she was afraid she'd offended him by mentioning his brother's prison record.

She needn't worry. His brother was a fine man, and Torque was not ashamed.

Kelly's fingers felt slender and cool as they disappeared in his rough grasp. His throat tightened even more. He looked away so she wouldn't see the tic of his eye.

"Well, um, would you have time, and would you be able to give me an estimate on fixing my car?" She gave a little laugh. "And check Mr. Hormel's car, too?"

Tough jerked his head up. "No." His gaze skidded across her, avoiding her startled look, and focused on the damages. He'd seen Kelly around. A lot. That bright yellow car was hard to miss. No one else around here drove a hybrid, either. Especially not a Cadillac hybrid. He'd heard, from the rumor mill, that the car was a gift from her fiancé.

Tough didn't know how that fiancé thing played out, exactly. But he knew what she did with her spare time, the kids she helped and the money she spent on her own to ease the struggle of kids in this town. She wasn't paying him a dime for this.

He was saving to rent the other half of the warehouse so he could expand his shop, but he would do that without Kelly's money. She hadn't been born rich, although she was engaged to marry money.

"Oh." The smile slipped a little from her face before she fastened it back on, brighter. "Well, could you give me a recommendation for another shop?"

A car ambled down the street, the driver rubbernecking at the two banged up autos as it passed by.

Tough watched the brake lights come on as the car stopped at the stop sign at the intersection. She had misunderstood him. Somehow he had to find the words to correct her, then get them out of his mouth, or she was going to walk away from him.

"I can do it." It sounded more like a growl than actual speech to his ears, but at least the words were out.

The older gentleman walked closer and stood with his arms crossed. "He looks like he can handle it, but is a reputable company? I'd hate it if you got fleeced on top of what I've done."

Before Tough could react, Kelly stepped between the man and him. Her finger waved in the air and her little sandal with its skinny, pointy heel, stomped on the sidewalk. He could almost feel the head of steam building up inside of her. The side of his mouth tugged up. Slowly, like it was rusty.

"Tough Baxter has a reputation around town for excellence in body work. I didn't realize this was his shop at first, but I've heard only good things about him. His brother is a prodigy with motors. The whole Baxter family has the kind of intelligence that enables them to fix anything." She punctuated her words with her waving finger.

There was nothing slow about the movement of Tough's mouth this time. After he pulled his chin off the ground, both sides were smiling at her off-hand compliment. How could she know that about him?

"Oh, I'm sorry. I didn't know." The man stepped back. "I really need my car. I know I'm not in a position to make demands, but can he have it done quickly? Maybe by tomorrow?"

Kelly said, "That's asking a little much, I think."

"It'll be done," Tough ground out.

Kelly whipped around. "Seriously?" she hissed in a softly shouted whisper.

Tough didn't move. He couldn't. He'd never been this close to her before, although he'd seen her plenty of times from far away. Color infused her cheeks. Her lively eyes seemed to sparkle and snap. He could almost feel the tingling energy that surged off of her. Tempted to touch her, just to see if she would shock him like an electric fence, he resisted, keeping his arms folded over his chest.

He nodded slowly.

She tilted her chin, acknowledging his nod, then looked back at the older gentleman. "That's good with you?"

Reading people wasn't his strength. Heck, there wasn't much that was his strength. But he could fix cars. Or trucks. Or busses, bikes, boats. Heck, he could probably even do body work on a locomotive, not that he'd ever had the opportunity to try. So Tough wasn't sure what, exactly, Mr. Hormell was thinking as he huffed out a breath and took another look at his older model car.

"How much?" the man asked, rubbing his chin. "And when?"

Tough didn't have to calculate. The cost, time and complexity of the repair had automatically computed in his head when he'd first seen the accident. He couldn't tell about Kelly's car, just because he couldn't tell from this distance whether or not the headlight holder had cracked, or whether any pieces of the grill had punctured any part of the front end of the motor. Both of those things were common. And both would complicate repairs. He could do it. It would just take longer. He still wasn't charging.

"By midnight," he said. After he fixed the dent, he'd have to spray primer and give it time to set before spraying the color-matched paint and then the clear coat. He gave an estimate on the price, grateful now that the shop had emptied out yesterday and he didn't have anything scheduled until tomorrow.

The man nodded. "Fine." He held out his hand. "Mr. Hormell."

Tough nodded and shook his hand.

Kelly bounced to the cars. "I can take you home, Mr. Hormell."

"No," Tough said. Hearing Kelly call him Mr. Baxter didn't sit right. But there was no way he was going to find the words to tell her about that.

She put a hand on her hip, planted her tiny sandals on the pavement and opened her mouth.

Tough didn't let her start. He forced his mouth open. "Don't drive it 'til I check it."

Took the wind right out of her sails. Her whole body deflated like a flat tire in summer. "Oh," she said meekly. She looked over at her car. "I guess something might be wrong with the motor or something..."

Yeah. And the Pope would ice skate in hell before Tough allowed her to drive away alone with a stranger.

He glanced toward Mr. Hormell. "I'll get them off." He nodded at the wrecked cars. "Then I'll take you."

He stopped in the act of turning away when cool fingers landed on his arm. A light touch, but a vice couldn't have stopped him faster. As much as he wanted, really wanted, to look down and meet her eyes, he just couldn't force himself to be that intimate. He set his jaw, angled his head so his ticking eye pointed away from her, fastened his eyes at a point over her left shoulder and waited.

"Could you...would you mind taking me to the shelter?"

She volunteered at the community activity center. It's where she got most of the kids she was always dragging around. But a part of him didn't want her to know that he knew so much about her. Experience had taught him that most people used their mouths more than their eyes and ears, and they expected the rest of the world to do the same. That same experience said that she would be freaked out, think he was a stalker, weird or worse, if she knew the facts he knew about her life and habits. Just from watching and listening. He breathed deeply through his nose. And now he had a scent to attach to all of that information. His arm burned. A scent, and a cool touch that scalded his skin.

He forced his eyes to meet hers for a fraction of a second before they skipped away.

"The community activity center on 15th street," she said slowly.

He was able to get his gaze to land on her dress, but couldn't quite meet her eyes. His eyebrow twitched.

"I volunteer there," she added.

"Yeah," he ground out, trying not to look like he knew. He wanted to tell her to wait, that he'd get the cars off the street and come back for her, but his back was turned and his feet were walking away, and his tongue never did unknot itself.

Chapter 2

Broad shoulders and narrow hips moved away from Kelly without a word of explanation. Should she follow him? She felt like an idiot just standing here. Being inactive, letting other people take charge, those weren't exactly traits that came naturally to her. But Torque's brother had left her with little choice. Torque, Tough...what odd names their family had. She had a vague recollection of hearing it before...somewhere. A memory teased at the back of her mind, but she couldn't catch the strand and pull it up.

She'd known Torque had a brother—she'd heard more than once from Cassidy what a mechanical whiz he was—but she hadn't known he was so...rugged. Quiet. Gruff. And obviously didn't want to be bothered by her.

Checking her messages again, although her phone hadn't buzzed or dinged, she sighed. No one had answered her. Cassidy was working. The ladies at the shelter were busy with kids. Her fiancé, Preston—how odd to finally think of him as her fiancé after practically growing up together—was probably busy, even though this was his day off. She glanced down at the new, very large, ring on her left hand. She had never said "yes" when he asked. He slipped the ring on like he'd known she was expecting it. Everyone expected them to get married, and she really did love him. Just a quiet love; no sparks or bells or whistles.

And his mother, Mrs. Fitzsimmons had done so much for Kelly. She was more of a mother than her own mother had been. How could she not marry Preston? Mrs. Fitzsimmons had been over the moon when Preston had finally announced their engagement. Everyone had been expecting them to get married, probably since high school.

She gave the ring a last look. It was pretty.

Marrying Preston would make Mrs. Fitzsimmons happy, but it didn't solve Kelly's problems. Like the fact that the community activity center had a roof that leaked, and the landlord kept promising to fix it, but refused to take the money and do so. Plus, it was across town, too far for most kids to walk, and she ended up driving around the city, picking them up and dropping them off every day. It was worth it to keep them off the streets, but it sure would be nice to find a suitable building in the area and open a new center. One that didn't leak every time it rained. Unfortunately the red-hot economy had the unanticipated consequence of snatching up available real estate.

Taking one last glance at her phone, she shoved it in her purse.

She looked back at her banged-up Cadillac hybrid. The kids in these neighborhoods needed her. She was making a difference in their lives, just as Mrs. Fitzsimmons had made a difference in hers. That was the most important thing to her. And if she had a few misgivings about the lukewarm attraction between her and Preston? She would shove them aside. Preston and she made a perfect match. Mrs. Fitzsimmons was happy and Kelly could keep working with the neglected and needy children in this town. That was really all that mattered.

Kelly hurried over to Mr. Hormell and offered her arm as he attempted to shuffle up the curb.

"Thank you, miss," he said.

She glanced over as Tough bent and lifted the garage door, the muscles in his back and arms bunching and stretching his tee. She clasped her hands together, trying not to remember the rough feel of his calloused hand closing around hers. It should have felt claustrophobic, as big and strong as it was. But it hadn't. It had felt warm and solid and right. A feeling that had surprised her.

Too bad the man couldn't seem to force himself to talk to her.

Tough climbed into Mr. Hormell's car and drove it slowly off the street and into his garage.

She smiled at Mr. Hormell and struck up a conversation about the weather, while wondering what it was about Tough that made her eyes want to follow his every move. It wasn't his charming personality; that was for sure. And there was something about him, something that nagged in the back of her head, like she'd known him before.

She forced herself to pay attention to Mr. Hormell as Tough strode back out and lifted the hood on her car. Had she ever seen a man with such a confident walk? His whole posture was loose and relaxed. Casual.

She was never loose or relaxed and she certainly didn't do casual.

Excusing herself from Mr. Hormell, she stepped quickly over to Tough and stuck her head under the hood. Maybe it was just an excuse to be near him, since she'd never actually seen anything that was under the hood of any car that she'd ever driven. Just like Preston had never seen her without her makeup armor.

"How bad are the damages?" Would she need to rent a car?

Tough pointed to the area around the headlight. "Cracked."

Kelly nodded, although she had no idea of what that meant. "That's bad?"

"Expensive." He shifted and a whiff of his manly scent drifted to her nose. Not expensive cologne or aftershave. Nothing like the way Preston smelled. But a mixture of grease and oil and gasoline under laid with a straight-up male potency. Were there male pheromones? Kelly tried to remember from the one science class she'd taken in college. What else could explain this odd pull that had her breathing deeply and stepping closer?

"Will it take long to fix it?" Her voice held a freak husky note. She swallowed to try to get rid of it.

"Order parts." Tough lifted his head, but again, his eyes looked past her, before he ducked back down and shifted away. Why wouldn't he look at her?

What did 'order parts' mean anyway? Maybe some kind of mechanic slang. She wasn't going to pretend she understood. "You can fix it, but you don't have the parts?"

"Yeah." He didn't look up that time, but kept his gaze on his hands which disappeared under some long, flat black thingy. He manipulated a plastic lever and something rattled, deep and low.

"That didn't sound good."

Tough shook his head. After checking several other places, he straightened and pulled a blue rag out of his pocket, wiping his hands. Kelly found herself fascinated with his short, black nails and long, agile fingers.

"Better tow it," he said.

"Can you fix it? Should I tow it somewhere that specializes in hybrids? Or Cadillacs?"

His hands stilled. She got the feeling he was using great effort. Maybe to keep from getting offended that she suggested someone else fix it?

"I can. Your choice." His words were short. Staccato, even. He shoved the rag into his back pocket. His eyes stared over her shoulder like he didn't give a flip what she chose.

She glanced at her phone, as if Preston would have magically texted her the answer. As if he'd even care where she got his car fixed.

She adjusted her purse strap over her shoulder and looked up. Tough's gaze landed on hers for a moment. Dark brown, swirled and layered like an expensive walnut floor. The zap from that brief eye contact ripped down her backbone and ricocheted back from her fingers and toes. She blinked. In that short flash, his gaze was gone, once again pinning something over her shoulder. His face, all sharp angles, except for the bump on his nose—evidence it was once broken—angled away from her.

"If you can fix it, I want you." That rogue, husky note had crept back into her voice. To her ears, it sounded sultry, like she was on the other end of a 900 number. Which was ridiculous. She was a doer, a worker, as befitted the wife-to-be of a lawyer and aspiring politician. But not sultry. Not seductive. And definitely not sexy. She couldn't spend hours every day in front of a mirror getting her hair and makeup just right when there were children who needed her.

Tough stood with his hand on the hood of her car, waiting for her to step back so he could close it. Without giving him another glance, she hurried over to Mr. Hormell.

"He's going to get my car off the street, then he'll take us to your hotel."

Tough hadn't said any such thing. But Kelly wasn't going to wait around while he got over whatever chip he had on his shoulder and managed to tell her what he was doing. She'd make it up, first.

Mr. Hormell pulled a handkerchief out of his pocket and wiped at the sweat that rolled on his forehead. After seeing his flushed face, Kelly took his arm. "How about we move over there to the shady side of the building?" she suggested.

He nodded and allowed her to lead him around where the temperature was noticeably cooler. Kelly willed Tough to hurry. Not because she was in a rush, which she was, she always was, but because Mr. Hormell needed to be back in the air conditioning. Despite being late May, the central Pennsylvania humidity made the actual air temperature feel like the south side of hell.

A rumbling caused her to turn her head back toward where they had been standing. Tough's tow truck, which looked to be older than Kelly, puffed black smoke and rumbled as he backed it slowly toward the front of her car. Tough hopped easily from the cab, his limbs sure and strong. His ball cap shaded those dark, walnut eyes, but Kelly stared anyway. For the first time, she saw in him a glimpse of the little boy he might have been. A boy like one of the many she worked with every day. He'd have been adorable.

Again, that feeling like she knew him, or should know him, hit her. Had she known him when they were younger? Back before Mrs. Fitzsimmons took her in? That seemed right, but she still couldn't remember. She squinted, studying his angled chin. He definitely had a strong profile. Quite handsome.

He glanced up and she whirled away, guilty. There was no law against looking at someone, but now, from the way she jerked around, he'd have to know she'd been staring. Wonderful. And why? No reason other than those stupid pheromones. She remembered reading about them, but didn't remember the antidote. Onions, probably.

Her eyes bounced then settled on the door on the far side of the building. Was that a For Rent sign? She checked Mr. Hormell, whose color had improved. "I'll be right back."

She hurried down the sidewalk to the door. Yep. For Rent. She punched the number from the sign into her phone and hit the green button. With her phone to her ear, she peered in the dirty glass.

A counter, a couple of broken stools and a few partitions, some with holes that looked like they'd been punched.

Still. This location was perfect. So much closer to where all the kids lived. As long as the roof didn't leak, it would be perfect in every way. In fact, she glanced at her phone—not quite time for school to let out—some of the kids probably hung out on this very street. She picked up four girls and a little boy just two blocks over every day in the summer and took them to the children's center across town.

She tried the door knob as the phone went to voice mail, not expecting it to open. It didn't twist—it was locked—but the latch hadn't caught and the little bit of pressure she exerted had the door swinging in like the building wasn't quite square.

Her surprise had her hesitating as she started her message. "Um, hi. I'm Kelly Irwin. I'm interested in the building you have for rent on..." She looked back at the road sign, unsure what street she was on. Finding the street name she read it off, then rattled on, leaving her number.

After pushing the red "end" button, she stepped into the warm, dark interior, not really intending to trespass, but hoping to see if the building would suit her purposes.

The placed smelled musty and slightly tangy, like someone had left their dirty, wet socks lying around. Dust particles floated thickly in the light that angled steeply in from the side window. Kelly walked farther back, noticing the stools, the pages of designs, an old needle. The last renter had maybe been a tattoo parlor. She moved back, around the partitions. Whatever equipment they used to administer a tattoo had been removed. Just papers, trash and some broken pieces of plastic and other junk littered the floor.

She squinted at the ceiling. No drooping insulation or crumbling drywall. She glanced around. No wet patches on the floor.

She walked farther in. She could go right to negotiations about the price and length of lease if she already knew it would work.

With the partitions removed, there might be enough room for a basketball court. Sports were always good to keep kids involved and interested. But it couldn't be everything to a child.

She bit her lip as an old memory shimmered through her mind. It had been forever since she'd thought of her real parents. She never knew her dad. Her mother hadn't been interested. How Kelly survived as a baby and toddler, she'd never know, since she couldn't remember her real mother ever caring whether she was home or fed or clean or anything. Memories of being alone and scared, of having no one who cared and no place to go are what drove her now.

Thankfully, back then, someone had wanted a little girl.

The image wavered in her mind. Her heart stumbled, and she stopped short in the dim interior.

Now she remembered where she knew Tough from. Of course. How could she have forgotten? He was the little boy who had taken her by the hand and led her little five-year-old self to Mrs. Fitzsimmons, Preston's mom. He didn't talk back then, either. She wasn't sure she even knew his name back then. And she hadn't seen him much after that.

Shaking her head, she walked deeper into the dark interior. Tough didn't seem to remember her. But she would always owe him for what he'd done. After all, if it hadn't been for Tough and Mrs. Fitszimmons, who knows where she would have ended up with her dad completely gone and her mom drunk and high most of the time. Whatever the scenario, her mom didn't have time for Kelly. It was hard and hurtful as a child, but it made it a lot easier to relate to the kids she worked with now.

The darkness had gotten thick, so she fumbled with her phone to get the flashlight app up. Once the bright light cut through the darkness, she could see there was nothing much different on back. A door with a sign that indicated there was a restroom. She didn't even want to go there.

Another door. Curious if the space was wider than the open waiting and reception area, she tried this door. Unlocked, but stuck. She shoved. It moved enough to encourage her to gear up for a harder, quicker shove. Leaning her shoulder into it, and planting her feet, she bent her knees and rammed it hard.

The door stuck for a second, then opened in a burst of light and potent male air. She'd been expecting the burst, and was prepared. However, the pointy heel of her sandal had not, apparently, been designed as sturdy as a B&E attempt required. It twisted and snapped, sending Kelly reeling, off-balance, head-first into a well-lit office, and stumbling into the steel-like rigidity of Tough Baxter's arms and chest.

Thanks so much for reading!

To order Tough Talk, click here[1].

KELLY IRWIN JUST WANTS to help children like she used to be—underprivileged, hungry, and with a family so mixed up she wasn't sure who she really belonged to. None of them wanted the responsibility to raise her. She's convinced herself that she loves her fiancé and that they'll make a great team.

Tough Baxter is trying to establish his business and keep his side job a secret. After all, most people don't think that a man who can barely string two sentences together in the presence of a woman would make a very good relationship advice columnist. Then Kelly moves her children's center next door to his garage and suddenly not only are his plans to expand his shop wrecked, but his secret is in danger of being exposed.

After spending time with Tough working and helping kids, Kelly can't deny the attraction she feels for the soft-spoken mechanic. But she has a fiancé and a life plan which doesn't include Tough, so she turns

---

1. https://www.amazon.com/Jessie-Gussman/e/B076Z45PDV/ref=sr_ntt_srch_lnk_3?qid=1544733275&sr=8-3

to the advice columnist all of America is writing to. Will he tell her to follow her heart or pursue her dream?

Acknowledgements

The Lord has been so good to me. I've been blessed so much beyond what I deserve.

Thank you to my husband and children for allowing me to disappear with my laptop. I especially need to thank my oldest daughter. We called it "home ec" and gave her a credit for it (I love homeschooling!) but she shouldered the burden of this crazy household so I could write, and I'm grateful.

I wouldn't be publishing this without my Critique Partner, Carlyn Jones. She's the best.

Interestingly, I'm the only American in my critique group. Ramla Zareen, Kimberly Dallaire, Iris Darshi and Lydia have so much talent and a ton of patience and put up with this stubborn Yankee. It's a great group of ladies, and I don't deserve to be a part of it. Thank you!

Victorine Lieske did the cover from a picture Frank Scott took of one of our trucks while it was sitting in our driveway. They are both amazing.

Jenny Proctor and Peter Senftleben, editors, are extremely talented and both helped me with content editing. All mistakes are my own.

More books by Jessie:
The *Sweet Haven Farm* Series:
Book #.5 (a novella) Harvest Moon Homecoming[1]

[2]

WHEN THE HIGH SCHOOL'S float explodes five days before the National Farmer's Day parade, Principal Calvin Finkenbinder sees his chance at the promotion to Superintendent disintegrate. Unless he enlists the help of Ellie Bright, the most annoying, disorganized and kissable woman he knows.

Standing in Principal Fink's office, again, for driving her daughter to school late, again, Ellie is given two odious choices. Either her straight A daughter receives detention for another tardy that's not her fault, or Ellie uses her artistic skills and helps the uptight, stringent principal build a new float.

As they scramble to construct the float in time, Ellie's chaotic life collides with Fink's methodical plans. A tangle of arguments and decorations leads to a stolen kiss. Underneath their long established animosity is an unexpected passion that threatens to ruin more than just a school float.

1. https://www.amazon.com/gp/product/B076HP2L1K/ref=dbs_a_def_rwt_bibl_vppi_i2

2. https://www.amazon.com/gp/product/B076HP2L1K/ref=dbs_a_def_rwt_bibl_vppi_i2

Book #1 *Better Together*[3]

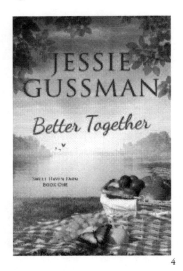

[4]

---

3. https://www.amazon.com/gp/product/B07DBF4X3H/ref=dbs_a_def_rwt_bibl_vp-pi_i0

4. https://www.amazon.com/gp/product/B07DBF4X3H/ref=dbs_a_def_rwt_bibl_vppi_i0

He wants her to notice him. She has to pretend she doesn't.

World Champion snowboarder, Wyatt Fernandez, should be starting his job as a ski instructor in the Andes. But an emergency means he has to spend the summer on his step-family's tree farm with his step-cousin and best friend, Harper. She's too busy with her books and getting tenure to notice he's wanted more than friendship for a long time.

Homebody and nutritionist, Dr. Harper Bright, must give up her summer research position so she can help on the family tree farm. With Wyatt. He might push her out of her comfort zone, but he's always "gotten" her. But she doesn't want to scare off the best friend she's ever had just because Wyatt is suddenly far more interesting than the nutritional benefits of broccoli. In order to keep their friendship intact, she has to pretend she's not infatuated with her best friend.

But when Wyatt names Harper as his fiancé to appease his dad who's pressuring him to return to Chile early, he never dreams Harper might actually have to play the part. Wyatt wants more than a reluctant fake fiancé. He has one last summer to convince Harper that they're better together.

Book #2 *Just Right*[1]

---

1. https://www.amazon.com/gp/product/B07K8Z31YY/ref=dbs_a_def_rwt_bibl_vppi_i1

2. https://www.amazon.com/gp/product/B07K8Z31YY/ref=dbs_a_def_rwt_bibl_vppi_i1

Sometimes a match that's all wrong, turns out to be just right.

While waiting to audition for a rare tubist seat opening, Avery Williams intends to cheer up her cancer ridden neighbor. She plans a throwback Christmas party in the barn where the sick woman got engaged forty years ago. It will be the highlight of the year, unless the building gets destroyed first.

In town for a short while to help his sick mother, Gator Franks expects to grab a side job and make some quick cash to help pay her hospital bills. Unfortunately, he has to get past the ugliest cat he has ever seen, which happens to be attached to a little blonde with sparkling pink fingernails, a city-girl attitude, and a fixation on saving the barn he just contracted to tear down.

Slowly, using simple words, Avery explains to the uncouth mountain man—the one with the ferocious, tuba-player-eating dogs—that she can't have a party in the barn if he tears it down first!

When circumstances force them to work together, their attraction ignites. Can they give in to the growing feelings between them?

Don't miss out!

Visit the website below and you can sign up to receive emails whenever Jessie Gussman publishes a new book. There's no charge and no obligation.

https://books2read.com/r/B-A-HJJH-DMQW

BOOKS2READ

Connecting independent readers to independent writers.

Also by Jessie Gussman

Baxter Boys
What He Wants

Watch for more at jessiegussman.com.

About the Author

About the Author

Jessie Gussman lives on a farm in rural Central Pennsylvania with her husband, kids and a permanent guest or two. She writes sweet, contemporary romance with humor and heart.

To find out more about Jessie, check out her website.

For weekly updates on her latest books, deals on sweet romance and other exclusive content, sign up for her weekly Reader Group News.

Jessie is active on Twitter: @jessiegussman
Facebook: @jessiegussmanwrites
Read more at jessiegussman.com.